Lock Down Publications and Ca$h Presents

CARTEL MONEY: COUP D'ETAT

By
Martell "Troublesome" Bolden

Lock Down Publications
P.O. Box 944
Stockbridge, GA 30281
www.lockdownpublications.com

Like our page on Facebook: Lock Down Publications
www.facebook.com/lockdownpublications.ldp

Stay Connected with Us!

Text LOCKDOWN to 22828 to stay up-to-date
with new releases, sneak peaks, contests and more…
Or CLICK HERE to sign up.
Like our page on Facebook:
Lock Down Publications: Facebook
Join Lock Down Publications/The New Era
Reading Group
Visit our website:
www.lockdownpublications.com
Follow us on Instagram:
Lock Down Publications: Instagram
Email Us: We want to hear from you!

PROLOGUE

Nightfall shrouded the parking lot of an abandoned factory, where Peso, along with Juan and Raul, awaited to meet with the connect. The trio were sitting inside of the smoke grey Range Rover HSE which was parked. Raul sat behind the steering wheel while Juan occupied the passenger side and Peso took up the backseat with a tote bag containing stacks of cash on one side of him and a Draco on his other. They had picked up where Peso's father had left off in the game.

Nearly a year had passed since Peso and his family was devastated by the murder of his father Luis. As an immigrant from Mexico, he could not seem to find work in the U.S., so Luis opted for the illegal work and set up a drug operation on the south side of Milwaukee. And the operation lasted for years, until a rival drug trafficker eventually blew out the brains of Luis in front of plenty of people—including Peso—to make a point.

Even before his father's death, Peso had a reputation for flippin' drugs and shootin' it out with the opps. But witnessing his dad be murdered turned him ruthless.

"Peso, you aight, or what?" Raul inquired, glancing at him through the rearview mirror.

"Uh, yeah. Yeah, I'm aight," Peso responded, losing his train of thought. "I was just thinkin' about my dad. That's all."

"Don't trip, lil bro. We gon' get even," Juan assured. "Just remember all the shit that he taught us in this game."

"Luis was somethin' like a dad to me also," Raul added. He had known Luis since his preteen years.

"Still can't believe that that puta smoked my dad right in front of me. Can't wait until I finally run into him, then it'll be his time to die," Peso asserted.

"Had any of our shooters spotted his ass, then he would definitely be dead by now," commented Raul.

Peso planted and caressed the Draco beside him and replied, "Good thing they hadn't, 'cause I want the chance to personally shoot that puta dead."

"And you'll get the chance soon enough," Juan told him.

"The sooner the better. Then, afterwards I'll be able to have my mind on money instead of on murder." Peso knew that there was lots of money to made. His gang was getting loads of marijuana and heroin from the connect, and their operation was growing vastly.

The pearl white Mercedes-Benz C300 that had just pulled into the lot was owned by the connect, Cobra. He was accompanied by two of his men, Ambrose and Suave, who worked for the kingpin.

On the south side of the city, Cobra was the recognized kingpin and the principal plug there for anyone dealing in Za and H. Peso began obtaining product either directly from Cobra, or through Suave.

Stepping out of the Range, Peso and the others were prepared to take care of business. The Benz braked to a stop in the parking lot and in the night Peso nem were milling around in front of the headlights of the Range which was parked near the abandoned building. As Cobra and his men walked up to the group, Ambrose recognized Luis's son and immediately realized that he was being alley-hooped to the opps, since he was the one who had murdered Luis. Peso upped his Drac' on Ambrose, then Juan and Raul followed suit. Ambrose understood that if he attempted to draw the Glock on his waist, before he could reach its handle, he would be shot dead.

Ambrose eyed Cobra perplexed and uttered, "So this is how you gonna do me, Cobra, after I was the one who made you who you are?"

"You did this shit to yourself when you decided to steal from me," Cobra hissed. He peeped how Ambrose seemed caught off guard. "What Ambrose, thought I wouldn't find out about it? Well, this is what happens when you cross me."

The streets that Cobra came to dominate was once under the control of Ambrose, who used to be one of the most prominent hustlers in the city. He had brought Cobra into the Mexican Cartel. Ambrose first employed Cobra as a mule to smuggle small caches of drugs into the United States from Mexico, but soon began trusting him with deliveries of heroin and weed as far as California. Cobra was bright and ambitious. During his trips to Cali and other big cities, he began to realize that the market went beyond the vision of the boss. After working a few years under Ambrose's tutelage, Cobra began making separate deals with Ambrose's customers and soon forged connections with other buyers. Before long, he was operating an enterprise that was completely independent of Ambrose's. Over time, Cobra also managed to get plugged with Ambrose's suppliers in Mexico.

Ambrose, meanwhile, had suffered reverses when several valuable drug shipments were busted coming across the border and those financial misfortunes were so devastating that he ended up seeking work from Cobra, his former worker. Eager to reestablish himself, Ambrose needed capital so he stole some money from Cobra's stash house. But he made the mistake of bringing a bitch with him to acquire the money, and she told Cobra about the theft during pillow talk.

With stares of death, Peso and Juan and Raul eyed Ambrose. He hastily spun on his heels running for his life in a desperate attempt to escape an inevitable death. Peso and the others chased him down while bustin'.

Rrraaa-rrraaa-rrraaa!
Boom-boom-boom-boom!
Boc-boc-boc-boc-boc!

Ambrose was shot several times in the legs and spine. He staggered and fell face down. The wounded and helpless man pled for his life while Peso, Juan and Raul stood over him unmoved by his pleas.

"P-please don't... take my l-life. Please!" Ambrose begged through rugged breaths.

"It's a life for a life," Peso remarked cynically. He aimed the Draco down on Ambrose and shot him to death.

Rrraaa!

Afterwards, all of the men stood around passing a blunt of Za. When the blunt was done, they buried the body of Ambrose, exchanged the cash and drugs, then got into their perspective vehicles and parted ways.

The murder of Ambrose vindicated Peso while it sealed Cobra's control over the streets, which in due time would belong to Peso.

CHAPTER 1

Glasses filled with Tequila, some stacks of cash, and a few semiautomatics was on the table which Peso was seated at with Juan and Raul. Their table was located near the rear of the restaurant.

They were at Peso's tawdry restaurant in one of the buildings on South National Street. It was called Lu's, after his father. The place specialized in cabrito, roasted baby goat, and was a favorite rendezvous in the early afternoon for local hoodlums. He also did a lot of business there.

In his late twenties, Peso possessed Latin features with a baby face that had a shadow of a mustache and only a fuzzy chin; his fine hair was cut low with deep brush waves; his roguish grin revealed the lower row of his teeth dipped in gold; he had a bronze hue with a collage of tattoos covering each arm and he was on the shorter side with a trim build. As a teen, he was given the moniker Peso due to him being half Mexican and all about money. And to boot, he was down to shoot it out for respect.

Peso was making sure that his crew understood their roles in receiving the incoming shipment of ten kilos of heroin that was expected to arrive in the next few days. He had the cargo coming in directly from Mexico through one of Cobra's couriers with the hopes that it slips by U.S. Customs near the border.

"Be sure you at the location when the load shows up to see that it's all there," Peso instructed Raul.

"I'll be there," Raul assured. He was the right hand man of Peso. Chubby with long hair that he normally wore in two braids and a pair of piercing gray eyes, Raul carried himself with stoicism and would kill at will.

"Once the load check out, then see to it that the product is taken to the stash house."

"No problem."

Peso looked to Juan and said, "Get the hustle fee together and pay it to Cobra so we'll be able to move the product without bein' harassed by the DTF." As long as Peso remained under Cobra's wing, he was guaranteed his immunity in exchange for a payment to the Drug Task Force.

"I'll handle it," said Juan, who then took a swig from his glass of 1800. He was actually Peso's older brother. He was baldheaded with a rotund belly and a bronze complexion. Juan was humorous while at the same time recklessly murderous.

Entering the restaurant, Tyson noticed that the only ones present were Peso and his boys. He was there to conduct some business with Peso. Being hooked on heroin, to support his habit, Tyson supplied a number of addicts and was a capable of moving a brick of boy in a week. He was a young white, bone thin guy with track marked arms from using heroin filled syringes.

"Peso, how's things going?" Tyson greeted as he took a seat in the only vacant chair at the table.

"Things are good, as long as you brought my paper," Peso replied.

"Don't I always." Tyson produced a wad of cash and sat it atop the table in front of Peso. "There's your money. Now where's the good stuff?"

Peso pushed the takeout bag with an ounce of heroin inside of it across the table towards the dope fiend, and said, "There's more where that comes from."

"I'll be in touch." Tyson collected the takeout bag and headed for the exit.

After servin' Tyson, Peso asked Juan and Raul to ride along with him to go and see he and Juan's mother. They each grabbed their pistols from the table, then exited Lu's and piled into Peso's silver BMW X6 SUV.

Lil Poppa's "H Spot" played as the Beamer truck wove through traffic. The south side of the city residents were predominantly Black and Hispanic. The area was crime infested where robberies, drug trafficking, and gangland murders were common occurrences. Most of the residents did not report crimes due to either not trusting the police or fear of retaliation.

Arriving at his mother, Tamera's place, Peso parked at the curb out front. She lived in a handsome home with a nice lawn that was located in South Milwaukee, which Luis had bought them. Out of respect for Tamera and her home, Peso and the others decided to leave their poles in the whip. Although, Tamera was aware of the lifestyle they lived.

Tamera was a beautiful black woman who prided herself on being a good mother and wife. Pushing fifty years of age, she looked damn good with her brown complexion and curvy figure. More than anything, she loved her children.

"Hey boys," Tamera greeted the trio once she opened the front door. She pecked each of them on the cheek as they entered. "It's nice that you boys came to see me, since I haven't seen you in days."

"Our bad, Ma. We just been busy," Peso said.

"Too damn busy to come see your own mother?"

"Ma, it's not even like that," Juan piped in.

Raul added, "We love seein' you whenever we can."

"Well, make sure to come see me more often." Tamera took a seat on the couch. "If you're hungry, I made something to eat."

In a hurry, Juan and Raul headed into the kitchen. The food at Lu's was good, but it did not compare to Tamera's home cooked meals. Peso decided to skip the meal and took a seat on the couch beside his mother.

"Ma, I want you to have this." Peso pulled out a wad of cash from the front pocket of his Amiri jeans and handed it to her.

"Lupe," she began, addressing him by his first name. "You don't have to give me money. Your dad left me with more than enough to take care of myself."

"But I want to give it to you, 'cause I'm just doin' what my dad used to." Ever since his father was killed, Peso and his brother did what they can to take care of their mother.

Tamera sighed. "That's what I'm afraid of." She shifted towards him in her seat. "Lupe, what your dad used to do is what got him killed. And I don't want the same thing happening to you or your brother. Especially with you having your girlfriend and daughter."

"Believe me, my girl and baby are important to me. As for my dad, I'm sure he would be proud of his sons," he told her, leaving out the detail of having avenged his father. He stood just as the others returned to the front room. "Ma, we'll come to see you again soon, but we gotta go take care of some business."

After each of them hugged Tamera, they left out. The three returned to the BMW and, before pulling off, they grabbed their blicks. Peso nem understood that being ready to bust at any given moment in the street life would make the crucial difference between life or death.

They rode to a couple of H spots to collect profits, then took it the stash house. Afterwards, Peso dropped off Juan and Raul at their places of choice. Following a long day of taking care of business in the streets, Peso was on his way home. He gripped the Glock .45 that was in his lap as he steered the Beamer. It being night out, he had on the headlights to help lead the way through traffic.

Once Peso reached his neighborhood located in a pleasant area, he spun the block twice to be sure no one was tailing him. Then, he went through the alley and parked inside of the garage that was behind his house. He lived in a nice brick house with his longtime girlfriend Mona and their five year old daughter Maxine.

Peso entered the house through its rear door. As he made his way into the front room, he came upon Mona carrying Maxine, who was sound asleep, into her bedroom. He went to help tuck in his sleeping beauty, then gently pecked her on the forehead. She was the spitting image of her daddy with her mommy's fair skin complexion. Peso and Mona practically tiptoed out of the room so not to awake their baby girl. They then stepped into the master bedroom they shared.

Mona laid in their king-sized bed atop the covers. She was a gorgeous fair skinned Mexican woman. Her hair was long and dyed red, along with her arched eyebrows. Her frame was petite and curvy. She was pleasant with lots of Latina flare.

"I'm glad that you're finally home. Maxie fell asleep while trying to wait up for you," Mona said.

"I'on mean to be out all day, but it get that way at times when I'm in the streets handlin' business," Peso replied as he removed the .45 from his waistband and placed it inside the top drawer of the nightstand on his bedside.

"I understand, which is why I look forward to you coming home after long days like this one." Mona was aware of his street affairs, and she hardly complained about it. Because it was the way he was able to pay for their house, her red Lexus IS, and the boutique she managed.

Climbing out of bed, Mona stepped to Peso and began kissing his lips. He held either side of her slim waist and returned her kiss. The couple helped one another undress. Once they were nude, Peso sat Mona on edge of the bed; he knelt in between her legs and planted his mouth on her pussy.

"Mmm... yes, papi. It feels so damn good," Mona moaned as he flicked his tongue rapidly over her clit. She palmed his wave covered head and watched him suck, lick, and slurp on her twat. It felt amazing when he sucked her clit while he finger-fucked her at the same damn time. "Oh, my goodness, I'm finna cuuum!"

Peso rose to his full height, then kissed Mona and allowed her to taste her own pussy juices. He used the tip of his hardness to play with her twat and, just as she was reaching climax, he slid every inch of himself deep within her. "Damn girl, you feel so fuckin' right," Peso groaned as her pussy creamed his dick. He watched his dick slide back and forth in her wet shot as he stroked her.

It was not long before Mona felt herself about to cum again. She was laid back in bed with her legs agape while Peso filled her with his large wood. "Yaaas, that's my spot," she purred out of pleasure. "Fuck me just like that, papi."

"I'ma fuck you just the way you want me to." Peso began to hammer her pussy, causing Mona to arch her back off the bed. He felt her warm juices slide down his inner thighs as she had an orgasm once again. The shit turned him on so much that a nut began to swell in the tip of his piece. Some strokes later and he busted a nut. "Damn, baby!"

The two lie in bed, drained from the quickie. Mona dozed off while he caressed her thigh. Soon, he too had fell asleep. Peso never wanted to bring heat to where he lay his head, because he wanted to sleep soundly at night, free of fear of arrest or death.

CHAPTER 2

On 27th and Greenfield Street, the black Lincoln Navigator braked at the stoplight. Suave was pushin' the SUV while Peso rode shotgun. They were on the way to make a serve on behalf of Cobra. Suave and Peso often did business together.

"Peso, we've came far since bein' in the Feds together. Now we're in these streets makin' shit happen," Suave mentioned.

"Yeah. Good lookin' for helpin' me get right back into the game when I got out," Peso said, then puffed the blunt of Za.

"It's nothin', my boy."

When Peso was in jail on a drug charge, Suave was one of his most important jail friends. They met in federal prison. Suave had arrived at prison nine months after Peso began his sentence, but they were both released about the same time and continued their friendship. Suave had introduced Peso to Cobra, who handed Peso a machine gun and a brick of boy and put him to work. Peso, meanwhile, built his own operation. He hired runners to take loads for him and had Juan and Raul collect profits.

Suave, who took on the nickname from his debonair persona, had a jockey build, wore his hair cut into a bald-fade, and was Mexican. He distributed product for Cobra. As his importance to Cobra rose, Suave was trusted to deal with more of the kingpin's buyers and, more importantly, with his drug suppliers in Mexico. Eventually, he was handling the movement of drugs across the border.

"One thing fa sho," Suave went on, "I ain't never lettin' twelve throw my ass in a cell again."

"I'on know about you, but they'll never take me alive," Peso stated, then took a pull of the weed.

"I feel you. Good thing we don't have to worry about the cops too much," Suave mentioned.

They knew that Cobra was actually paying the captain of the DTF a monthly fee, a payoff that allowed him to conduct activities without fear of arrest. Usually, the DTF captain would protect his payer from rivals; other times he would not. If the captain arrested or killed the one with juice, it was because he had stopped making payments, or because his name had started to get too hot and the trapper had become a liability.

Peso hit the weed once more, then passed the blunt to his boy. "I'm lookin' forward to receivin' those bricks of boy from Cobra. Already got most of it gone," he said.

"The load should be here in the next couple of days, then you'll get what you have comin', Suave told him as he pulled off with traffic.

"Suave, why haven't you branched off and headed your own crew?"

"'Cause I'm in a good enough position within Cobra's crew. It don't matter who's in charge to me, all that matters is how things are operatin'," Suave expounded, then inhaled some weed smoke.

"That's some real shit, my boy," Peso.

Suave glanced over at him and said, "Plus, bein' the kingpin comes with friends and enemies alike comin' for your crown."

Soon thereafter, they arrived at the destination. It was a large family home. Suave drove through the alley and parked behind the house, and Peso made sure his .45 was cocked, just in case.

The home belonged to Salvador, a gruff, unkempt man who was a well-respected drug boss. He copped product through Cobra but ran his own crew and operation. Salvador was callous, he even once murked a courier just to take a load of marijuana because he was short of cash to pay for it. He was not the type to take lightly.

Stepping out of the Navigator, Suave and Peso approached Salvador, who was flanked by his two sons Junior and Ceaser. Peso knew Salvador's sons through mutual acquaintances.

"Where's Cobra? I was expecting to talk about some further business with him," Salvador mentioned.

"He couldn't make it so he sent me on his behalf," Suave replied. "Whatever business it is you have with him, if it's somethin' I can handle just let me know."

"I would prefer to talk directly with the one in charge."

"Understood. Now, let's get down to business at hand." Suave opened the rear door of the Navigator and exposed the numerous pounds of exotic weed.

Salvador looked to his sons and instructed, "Junior hand over the money, then you and Ceaser unload the product."

As Salvador's sons unloaded the marijuana, Suave counted up the cash. Once everything checked out on each end, Suave and Peso returned into the interior of the Navigator and took off.

"I'on know 'bout you, but Salvador nem tend to give me a bad vibe," Peso pointed out.

"It's just that with Salvador bein' older, he just don't have respect for us young niggas and how we run the game now," Suave reasoned. He glanced through the rearview mirror more so out of habit.

Peso scoffed. "Then, he need to learn to respect the game as it is, 'cause a young nigga like me will die for mine."

"I feel you on that, my boy."

While en route to go and meet with Cobra at one of the stash houses, Suave made a pit stop at the gas station on 13th and Lincoln Street where he pulled up to a gas pump. He and Peso placed their poles on their waists before stepping out of the SUV, then entered the station. Peso purchased a box of Backwoods blunts and Suave paid for some petrol.

On the way out, they were laughing at something Suave had said when a champagne-colored Audi A4 braked and its bumper slightly bumped into Peso. Instinctively, Peso reached for the .45 on his waist, but paused with a hand grasping its handle once he realized there was a woman behind the vehicle's steering wheel. When she hastily exited the car to check on him, he then noticed how bad she was. Peso admired her chocolate hue, brown eyes, full lips and sculpted cheek bones, and her petite curvy frame. She stood 5'1" and was around 135 pounds with a nice ass booty and body and was sprayed with tattoos. Plus, she had her hair and nails and mink eyelashes and arched eyebrows all done professionally. Damn, shorty lil chocolate ass bad, Peso thought as he removed his hand from his pistol.

"Boy, are you alright?" she asked out of concern.

"Yeah, I'm aight," Peso responded coolly.

"Good. Well, you need to watch where you're going."

"Says the girl who nearly ran me over."

"Just barely," she objected as she started to return to her car.

"Damn. So you just gon' commit a hit and run without at least givin' me your name? By the way, I'm Peso."

"Sierra," she replied, offering him her name in return. She observed how fine the nigga was and did not mind the idea of gettin' to know him. "How about I give you my IG also?"

After they exchanged contact info, Sierra pulled out into traffic as Peso returned to the Navigator, where Suave was pumping gas. Once Suave slid behind the steering wheel, then they went their way to the stash house.

CHAPTER 3

The courier was to bring back a load from Mexico. It was to be delivered to Cobra form one of his top connects, Tito. Once the courier was to get the load across the border, he would deliver it and collect his fee.

He crossed the international bridge easily, but when he was on the two-lane road in Texas which linked Presidio with Marfa, the red lights of a police car flashed behind him, making his heart jump. The police ordered him out of the car and made him lean against the hood, both hands forward. They searched the car and found the load stashed inside of the door panels.

While the courier was being readied in Mexico with the load of heroin to deliver, someone across the border in Texas was tipping off American authorities. To save himself, the courier worked out a deal with the Drug Enforcement Agency.

***

"Hell do you mean he was busted?" Cobra had just received a call about his runner being arrested with the load. "Either someone tipped off the fuckin' cops or they just got lucky. Let's just hope he sticks to the code."

Ending the call, Cobra's thoughts were all over the place. He was confident that someone must have told the authorities about the delivery. How else would the cops know? He wondered if the courier would be able to keep his mouth shut. But little did he know, the courier had immediately given up information to the DEA that would cripple his drug operation. And now Cobra was out of a load of heroin that Tito had fronted him. However, Cobra still would have to pay for it.

Cobra understood the risks that came with the game. He was willing to do whatever he could to maintain on top in the game.

***

As Suave drove on 21st and Scott Street, he peeped through the sideview mirror and observed there was a maroon Dodge Magnum that had seemed to have been tailing him for at least a few blocks now. *Who the fuck could that be?* he wondered while attempting to squint through the suspect vehicle's tinted windows in order to get a good look at its occupants.

He had just come from collecting profits from a few of the trap spots, so he figured it could be some niggas who were out to rob him. Suave tightly gripped the Kil-Tec 9mm in his lap as steered with his available hand and perpetually glanced at each mirror. Once the Magnum's red lights began to flash, he realized it was the police.

Suave did not know if he was being pulled over for speeding or what. It would have been awfully hard explaining how an ex-con came by tens of thousands of dollars in the leather Prada satchel on the front seat; not to mention he was in possession of a firearm. His destination was only several blocks away, all he had to do was make a mad dash for the stash house. He gunned the Navigator and tried to outrun twelve, who was actually DEA.

The first corner he arrived at, Suave bent a hard right. Glancing into the rearview mirror, he observed the Magnum in pursuit of him. Approaching a yellow traffic light, Suave stabbed on the accelerator and sped through the intersection, narrowly avoiding collisions with other motorists. He still failed to lose the tail that was less than a block behind. Going back to prison was not an option for Suave as he drove recklessly through traffic during the high-speed chase. Committing a wide turn near Mitchel Street, Suave loss control of the Navigator and slammed into a light pole and totaled the SUV. The laws rushed onto the scene of the crash and expected to find a mangled body in the Navigator, but all they found besides the wrecked SUV was some traces of blood heading off into a gangway.

Suave had been thrown from the Navigator and had suffered a badly twisted ankle. His face and chest were scraped and bleeding. He managed to grab the satchel and gun from the truck, then hobbled away up to a duplex home that was a block over. He rapped on the door, and an elderly widower answered.

"Listen, ol' school," Suave said, gritting his teeth in pain. "I'll make it worth your while. Call my homeboy for me and tell him to come and get me. I'm hurt, and I'm hurt bad." He unzipped the satchel to show the stacks of cash inside of it, then the elderly gentleman hurried to grab his phone.

***

Salvador's luck ran out when the DEA surrounded his home. Salvador, his wife Maria, and their son Ceaser and his baby's mama, Yolanda, had just sat down to lunch when they heard the battering ram crash into the front door. With his family in the line of fire, Salvador had no intentions of putting up a fight. Hands in the air, he strode out of the front door, Ceaser right behind him. They were taken into police custody.

While the DEA was arresting Salvador at his home, agents had simultaneously arrested lots of his crew. Altogether, the DEA picked up fourteen people on the sweep. Most of the men, including Ceaser, were eventually released from custody within a several hours. Salvador, however, was charged with possession of more than a ton of marijuana that had been discovered in his garage.

It was apparent to Salvador that someone had snitched him out. Although, he would keep his mouth shut and accept his consequences.

***

Answering the knock at the door, Peso was aware that it was Tyson. Earlier Tyson had called and informed Peso that they needed to meet up in order to discuss some serious business, and Peso had instructed him to drop by Lu's Bar & Grille. Peso stepped aside for Tyson to enter, then locked the door behind him. They took a seat at one of the tables. Lu's was closed for the remaining of the evening so they had the place all to themselves.

"So, what's the deal?" Peso asked, getting down to business.

"The deal is that I have a guy who introduced me to a couple of good friends of his who are important buyers and needs a key of H. And since I don't have that kind of weight on hand, I figured that you could make the deal happen," Tyson said.

Peso leaned back in his seat. "And where do you know your guy from with the friends? How do I know that I can trust 'em?"

"My guy's someone I've been doing deals with for a while, and he assures me that his friend's cash is always good and they could be potential permanent buyers of yours."

"Listen, I'll deal with 'em. But since it's your deal, you have to get it done."

"I can do that. But they need the product by tonight. Can you make that happen?" Tyson wanted to know.

"I can make it happen. You just put the deal together," Peso told him.

Tyson stood and said, "I'll get in touch with my people, and then be back to see you."

After he departed Lu's, Tyson phoned the clients to let them know what was up. "Good news. My guy can take care of you right away. Let's meet up."

"Cool. Just name the time and place," the client replied in his raspy voice.

Half an hour later, two dudes pulled up to the gas station in a white Dodge Challenger Hellcat. Both stepped out drippin' in designer attire and rockin' jewelry bust-down with ice. Leon, one of the buyers, was dark-skinned and lean with a raspy voice. The other, Nate, was a short, stocky Hispanic with curly brown hair. They approached Tyson's whip and jumped in, Leon the passenger side and Nate the backseat.

"Lemme see whatcha got," Leon grunted.

Tyson showed the two a sample of the heroin and they observed it closely.

"Looks like some good shit," Nate commented.

"Trust me, it is," Tyson told them, having tested the dope himself. "Now, let me see the money." Nate showed him a stack of bills. "It's on. We'll meet you a few miles outside of town, at the truck stop. Wait for us near the highway. We'll be there in about half an hour."

Subsequent to meeting with Leon and Nate, Tyson had returned to Lu's in order to bring Peso up to speed. He was jumpy due to being nervous about the deal, and Peso peeped it.

"Sure you wanna go through with this deal?" Peso questioned. "'Cause you seem 'noid."

"Yeah, I'm sure. I'm just a little anxious, that's all," Tyson reasoned.

"The maybe you need somethin' to calm your nerves." Peso offered him a gram of boy and watched as Tyson wasted no time prepping the substance for consumption, then used a syringe to inject it into his frail, track marked arm. He could tell that the drug had Tyson at ease.

As they drove on the highway, Tyson was super relaxed. Peso pulled out a wrapped brick and put it on the middle console. Inside of the cellophane wrapping was a kilo of black-tar heroin that was dark brown and looked inoffensive as modeling clay. Since it was Tyson's deal, it was now Tyson's responsibility to hand the product over to the buyer and collect the money while Peso stayed at a distance. Peso only came along to get a look at the two buyers if they were going to potentially be in business.

They spotted Leon and Nate in the white Hellcat parked next to the entrance of the truck stop. Tyson turned into the lot and the Hellcat followed close behind. They parked near the semi-trucks and everyone got out of their vehicles.

It was late in the evening, and a chilly breeze was blowing. As Tyson walked up to the two buyers, Peso pulled his Milwaukee Brewers cap lower to cover his eyes. He leaned against the cab of Tyson's Chevy Malibu and watched over the hood. Usually, he was extremely careful about customers, dealing only with people he had known a while. He knew Tyson, he knew many other dealers. But this was his first time he had laid eyes on the two buyers.

Hopefully, this isn't a fuckin' mistake," Peso contemplated.

Tyson and the two buyers were standing at the rear of the Hellcat. Tyson flashed a smile as he handed over the brick to Leon. Nate used a pocketknife this cut a small slit in the package in order to check the product out and make sure they were getting what they were paying for. Nate took a pinch of the boy and examined it closely. Tyson knew it was good.

"The shit looks all good to me," Nate said.

"Then, where's the money?" Tyson urged.

"Don't trip, homey, we got it," Leon piped in. "I'll get the cash right now."

Tyson was always nervous at such moments, but also exquisitely happy. Brokering a deal meant a ten percent cut for him, and money meant a continuation of the opiate-induced serenity he craved. Now all that was left was for him to get the paper and get the hell out of there.

Leon popped the trunk where there was tote bag containing money, then Tyson bent down to pull the tote bag out. Just as Tyson moved closer to grab the tote bag, Leon shoved a police badge in his face and pointed a service weapon at him.

"D.E.A. You're under arrest, Tyson. Get your fuckin' face to the ground!" Leon ordered.

Peso upped the .45 Glock from his waistband when he saw the niggas shoving Tyson to the ground behind the Hellcat. He was ten yards away. Tyson's vehicle separated him and the other men; he could not hear clearly what the buyers were saying, but he realized somethin' was wrong when he saw Tyson abruptly straighten up. He saw a pistol in the hand of the dark-skinned nigga. It was happening so fast, Peso did not know what to think. Was it a robbery? Was it a bust?

If Peso even thought about bustin', he quickly changed his mind when he saw a DEA van barreling through the parking lot from the other side with of the lot. He turned and sprinted towards the semi-trucks, running in between them so fast that his cap blew off his head. He heard Nate shout, "Stop, or I'll shoot!" A shot rang out and Peso heard the bullet whing into the ground just in front of him. He kept running. He knew that if he was caught he would definitely spend the next twenty years in prison.

Nate sprinted after Peso. He could see Peso looking every which way as he closed the distance between them. When they ran behind the restrooms of the truck stop, the agent saw Peso turn and take aim with only a short distance separating them.

Boc-boc!

Nate had dropped to his knees and shot first. Peso took off again, and the agent lost him somewhere in the parking lot.

The rapidly approaching darkness and Peso's cunning nature saved him from capture. While an police airplane droned overhead, the authorities combed the area but before long it was too dark to see. They were sure he was still somewhere in the area, but any further searching would be reckless. He had a gun and it was clear he was willing to use it. The authorities called off the hunt.

Peso had gotten away, but unfortunately Tyson had been arrested and would be charged with the kilo of heroin. The DEA tried to get him to snitch on Peso but he refused to. They believed Peso was a much bigger fish than Tyson, because Peso had to be, directly or indirectly, getting his dope from Cobra, the untouchable drug honcho.

CHAPTER 4

Cobra and several of his drug associates were partying at Baddies strip club. While they were in the VIP section poppin' bottles and making it rain, strippers entertained the crowd of dope-boys. This was a private party.

Cobra was in the company of Hector, nephew of the powerful kingpin in Mexico, and one of Cobra's chief suppliers, Tito. Hector had flown into town in a private jet earlier in the day with three shooters to discuss funds that Cobra owed the Mexican drug boss. Hector was a trusted member of the Mexican Cartel who evidently knew how to take care of situations.

"I 'preciate the hospitality, Cobra. You always know how to make me feel welcomed," Hector said. He watched as a stripper performed pole tricks on the mainstage.

"What can I say, you're like family to me. You're welcomed to my city any time," replied Cobra, then he took a drink directly from his bottle off Casamigos.

"Good to know." Hector turned his undivided attention to Cobra and eyed him through slits. "Enough of the pleasantries, let's get down to the real reason I'm here. As you already know, my uncle sent me to collect his debt. Why have things been slow?"

Cobra shifted towards him in his seat. "It's tied to a financial crisis I've experienced due to a string of serious losses—major drug shipments that had been fronted to me by the jefe had been seized by the feds. The dope busts represents huge money losses for me." During the previous month, at least thirty bricks of Cobra's heroin and over a ton of marijuana had been confiscated in drug busts throughout the city.

Hector relaxed back in his seat and took a drink from his glass of Tequila while eyeing Cobra over its rim. "Sorry to hear that. However, you're still responsible and have to pay for those loads, and that's my purpose of visiting," he stated. "When are you going to make good on the debt?"

"Understood. And I have the cash for you right now." Cobra knew he had to satisfy the nephew of his source. He waved over Suave, who limped over on his bad ankle with a leather satchel in hand and sat it on top of the table in front of Hector.

Hector unzipped the satchel and took a look at the stacks of cash. "My uncle will be satisfied," he assured with a smile. "Now, how about we take some of these lovely ladies back to a hotel."

After handpicking the girls that they cared to entertain them for the remaining of the night, the gang of dope boys headed out of the club. While Cobra, Hector and their crews walked through the parking lot towards their whips, several masked gunmen emerged from between parked automobiles. One of the masked gunmen demanded the crowd to give up their cash and jewelry. Hector wasn't going for that shit. He pulled out his .9mm and aimed it at one of the masked men, but another grabbed him by the arm before he could bust. Hector pushed back to free his gun hand and started bustin'.

Blam-blam-blam-blam-blam!

Rrraaa-rrraaa!

Everyone started bustin' back and forth. Cobra and a stripper ducked beside a parked Benz just as one of the gunmen—of Hector's—fired a machine gun at him. Bullets narrowly missed Cobra, but one bullet struck him in the lower back. Cobra returned shots over the hood of the vacant Benz, one of the masked gunmen was hit in the arm and stomach from Cobra's Glock with a converter switch. During the gun battle, Hector was shot through the heart and died instantly. The shootout ended when someone in the parking lot shouted that twelve was coming and the remaining masked men fled.

By the time twelve arrived, everyone were able to escape. Some of Cobra's boys, including a hobbling Suave, had helped him to the car and rushed him to the hospital in the small town of Racine that was approximately forty minutes away. The bullet wound was not serious, it just needed to get cleansed and patched up. While Cobra was in the hospital, Hector's uncle, and Cobra's plug, Tito, called him.

"What happened to Hector?" Tito, who was in his seventies, demanded to know, speaking in rapid Spanish. Apparently Hector's shooters had immediately reported the unfortunate incident to the jefe.

"There's been a problema, Señor Tito," Cobra said in a saddened tone of voice, responding in Spanish. "Unfortunately, Hector has been killed. Some guys ambushed us and the shooting started." He gave an edited account of the shooting.

"It's very sad what happened to my nephew on the account of him coming to collect your debt for me. By the way, what about the money? Where is it?"

"I don't know, I gave it to him. I don't know what happened to it."

"Bullshit, Cobra!" the old man spat. "One of Hector's men says he saw you shoot my nephew. And he cannot recall any money being handed over to Hector."

"Señor, I assure you that I gave Hector your money. Maybe one of his boys took it," Cobra told him.

"Perhaps you took advantage of the unexpected confusion to shoot Hector, then you could clear your debt by claiming that you had already paid off the big debt you owed and don't know what happened to the money after all," Tito accused. "Well, you won't get away with what happened to Hector or my money! I'll be sure to send a small army of my men to your town with orders to kill you!"

Without warning, the jefe hung up the line in Cobra's ear. Cobra believed that the robbers could have taken the money, or even Hector's own shooters, given the fact that one of them had attempted to shoot Cobra. And perhaps now that Hector was dead, his shooters were using Cobra as a cover up. Either way, he understood how powerful Tito was and that the jefe's threat was dead serious. Therefore, Cobra planned to disappear for a while.

Treacherous himself, he suspected everyone else of sinister intent to assist getting him out the way so they could take over his position. He did not plan to say a word of where he would lie low to even his closest associates. Cobra hoped to be able to straighten things out with old man Tito, and soon.

***

When Cobra fled Milwaukee, the south side's underworld was in a state of flux. Cobra, Peso's source of heroin and marijuana, was on the run. Rumors flushed around town that two black SUVs full of Tito's men armed with heavy artillery were on the lookout for Cobra. Cobra simply abandoned the lucrative area. For a short time, one of Cobra's cousins was said to be runnin' shit, but he was soon arrested. The south side was up for grabs.

By default, the south side fell to Suave. His star in Cobra's crew began to rise after he evaded the

DEA in the high-speed chase through the streets. The accident that day left him with a permanent limp but his resourcefulness and daring nature earned Cobra's esteem—and a promotion. Cobra put him in charge of all of the trap spots. That changed after Cobra disappeared. Now, Suave was left in charge of the entire operation, and he was dealing with the drug boss Tito.

Pulling into the parking lot of Mitchel Park, Suave parked his Porsche truck beside the Ford F-150. He was there to have a conclave with the captain of the DTF; this would be their third time meeting up since Cobra's disappearance.

It being later at night, the park was scarce. Suave hopped out of his Porsche, and then jumped into the F-150's passenger side. Captain Danielson was sitting behind the steering wheel taking swigs from a bottle of cheap whiskey. He was bald with stubble on his cheeks and steel grey eyes. And as a cop, Danielson was a drunkard and as crooked as they come.

"How about a drink," Danielson offered.

"I prefer Tequila," Suave refused.

"More for me." The captain turned the bottle up to his lips. He peered at Suave and said, "So about the hustle fee. It's been nearly two months since Cobra's little vanishing act, and the unpaid balance is climbing. Cobra's not making his payments and is falling behind. So, someone—that means you—had better come up with the money. Or we will help the feds shut things down." When Cobra couldn't be located for the hustle fee, Suave got an official visit from the captain.

Suave caressed his goatee. "And how much does Cobra owe?"

"So far, eighty grand."

"Look I'on have that amount of money lying around to just pay. Plus, whatever dealings you originally had with Cobra shouldn't fall on me."

"However, since he's gone, now you're the one who's left in charge. So I expect for you to find a way to make monthly payments, just the same," Danielson's explained.

"I'll tell you what, you wipe Cobra's debt clean, then I'll begin makin' payments at ten Gs a month startin' today." For Suave, just starting to pick up the pieces of an organization abandoned by its chief, the original sum would be ruinous.

Danielson leaned back in his seat. "We have a deal. But if you miss a payment, I'll be forced to take action," he forewarned.

"All I ask is that you continue to allow us to move our product without interference. And alert me of any fed raids," Suave bargained.

"Fine. Just know that I'm in no position to prevent the feds from snooping into your business. But as long as you keep the bank rolling in, you won't have to worry about the DTF."

Suave pulled out a bankroll, then tossed it into the crooked cop's lap. "There's the first payment."

"You can expect a visit from me next month," Danielson said as Suave pushed open the door to step out the truck.

Suave returned to his Porsche, then he and the captain parted ways. Now that Suave had made the payment to Danielson, he was officially in charge of things. After all, he was the one generating the money now, not Cobra. Cobra had left him in an ambiguous situation and had not tried to contact him.

A few months had come and went with Suave being in power. Adding to his importance, he quickly got big in his own right. He soon had all the trappings of a kingpin—his own crew of trappers and road runners, and stash spots. The drugs were being delivered directly from México to Suave. Business flourished the moment he took over from Cobra. The money was rolling in. Suave was making his monthly hustle fee payments. Everybody was satisfied.

Everybody except Cobra.

***

Cobra turned the bottle of 1800 up to his lips and took a gulp of the Tequila. He used the backside of his hand to wipe away some liquor trekking down his chin. In his hotel suite, he was seated on the sofa looking at his iPhone, watching Suave, who was drippin' in water around his neck and wrists, hand counting a fifty racks as he talked shit about being in charge of things and how rich he was while going live on Instagram. There was plenty of comments and hearts sliding up the side of the phone screen.

Still in hiding from Tito, Cobra was out of town. For now, he felt the need to stay out of Milwaukee, knowing Tito's men were there on the lookout for him. He had attempted to contact the old man in order to sort things out, but Tito did not believe a word Cobra said. Partially, Cobra believed that someone had set him up. Over time, rumors began circulating that the strip club shootout was the results of a power struggle over the south side. Someone had wanted Cobra out of the way, and, of all people, he couldn't help but believe it was Suave.

Cobra had it out for Suave. He considered Suave a traitor. Suave had taken advantage of his self-imposed exile to grab what was rightfully Cobra's. It did not matter that Cobra had not trusted Suave enough to contact him and clarify the situation. It only mattered that Suave now considered himself kingpin of the south side of Milwaukee, that he was boasting about it and making money Cobra thought was his. Now Suave was going to pay for it with his blood.

Going live on IG himself, Cobra mugged the camera. "I wanna let Suave know that since he thinks he's in charge of my shit, then I'ma show him that he's not when I smoke his ass! I'm still the head nigga in charge!" he raved.

Cobra tossed the iPhone aside on the sofa after ending the video. He took a gulp of the 1800, and it burned going down. His girlfriend Venus, who had been asleep in the adjacent bedroom, had overheard Cobra ranting and came to check on him. She just cared to do what she could to comfort her man.

"Papi, is everything good?" Venus asked. She stood before him nude, her body looking amazing and her long hair falling down her back and some spilling over her shoulders.

Cobra huffed. "As good as it can be."

"Then, let me make it all better."

With no further words, Venus fell onto her knees and pulled his dick out of the Versace boxer-briefs he wore. He leaned back and took a swig from the bottle while she sucked his dick vigorously. Her mouth was warm and wet as she bobbed her head up and down in his lap orally pleasing him. She spat on his piece and gazed up into his eyes and moaned seductively while licking the tip of his hardness. She sucked his dick with no hands. Cobra enjoyed the feel of her luscious lips wrapped tightly around him. He felt himself nearly ready to bust a nut. Venus used a manicured hand to jack the shaft if his large dick while she sucked and licked his balls. She felt him tense up and knew he must be close to exploding. This encouraged Venus to perform on his wood with her mouth like she was in a porno. It wasn't long before Cobra grunted as his dick spit up semen, and Venus swallowed the cream.

Cobra still believed that revenge on Suave would make him feel even better.

CHAPTER 5

While Peso sat at the table with Raul in Lu's Bar & Grille, they were having drinks and discussing matters. Aside from the usual hoodlums, the establishment was occupied by some patrons enjoying the food. Suave entered Lu's, and Peso took notice to the newfound kingpin as he sat in a booth along with his shooter, Rock. Peso excused himself from the table with Raul in order to go over and speak with Suave.

Stepping over to the booth that Suave occupied, Peso took himself a seat opposite of him. Suave instructed Rock to go and grab himself a drink while he speak with Peso. The broad Brazilian man did as told and left the two be.

"How's business?" Suave inquired.

"Good. Been able to move product twice as much," Peso answered.

"As long as I keep the blue goons paid, then we can hustle without much interference."

"Well, here's my part of the hustle fee." Peso dug out a knot of cash from the pocket of his Off White jeans, then handed it to Suave. He respected Suave's position and would fall in line, unlike some others.

Suave pocketed the cash. "Good lookin'. You know, some guys still honor Cobra as the one in charge instead," he admitted bitterly.

"If Cobra had still been in charge of things, I would have paid him instead. There's laws in the game to be obeyed, but they're not the ones written down in the code books," Peso expounded.

"Now that I'm makin' the hustle fee payments, I'm in charge of shit. Cobra's no longer generatin' the money, I am. He left me in an indistinct circumstance and haven't tried to get in touch with me. So what am I supposed to do?" Suave asked. "If Cobra's not here to pay the hustle fee and they make me pay it instead, that means I have the south side and not Cobra. I'on owe him nothin'."

"I feel you on that." Peso rested his elbows atop the table. "Dawg, word is beginnin' to spread around that Cobra is plannin' to smoke you," he informed. "Listen, maybe you should just leave town for a while."

Suave leaned back in his seat. "Maybe you're right. I'll go down to Miami this weekend, and you should come with me. But I refuse to go into hiding like Cobra, 'cause I ain't duckin' him at all."

"I can respect that."

"Good." Suave stood. "I'll link up with you this weekend," he said, then dapped Peso. As Suave turned for the exit, his shooter Rock followed close behind.

***

Miami was full of beautiful weather, beaches and women. Peso, Suave and a few of his boys, including Rock, had spent a few days in the Sunshine State cashin' out and gettin' lit at some of the best spots. It was nice for a change to get away from the streets of Milwaukee so they could relax. With all of the raids and murders taking place, being able to unwind is what they needed.

During lunch, the gang of drug dealers occupied a table in a Colombian eatery. They ate meals and had drinks while talkin' shit among each other.

"Tonight is our last in Miami, so let's hit the club and do it big," Suave said, and the others agreed. "Even though I've enjoyed all that this beautiful place had to offer, it's time to get back home and back to the money."

"Yeah, you right. I have a lot of business to tend to back home," Peso piped in. He left Raul in charge of his operation.

"For now, let's get lit while we're in Miami."

Suave stopped a sexy ass young Colombian waitress and ordered his table bottles of Casamigo. Excusing himself, Peso headed towards the restroom. Subsequent to taking himself a piss and washing his hands, Peso was returning to the table when he was halted by a middle-aged Colombian guy who was well-dressed in a very expensive looking Tom Ford suit. Peso thought, *What the hell could this guy want?*

"Allow me to introduce myself," the stranger began in a humble manner. "My name is Manuel, and I am the owner of this fine establishment." He shook Peso's hand, and Peso peeped the Patek timepiece hugging the man's wrist.

"Peso," he replied averse, and the man smiled inwardly at such a name.

"I couldn't help but overhear you and your friends. Something tells me that you're dealers from out of town," Manuel told him. He could also observe that Peso and the others were drug dealers by their bust-down jewelry and how much cash they carelessly threw around.

"And, what's it to you?" Peso pressed.

Manuel chuckled. "I don't mean to slight you. Let's just say that I am a man of business with significant connects. Why don't you take my card and call me if you are interested in talking more." He provided Peso with a business card, and then moved along.

Continuing towards the table with thoughts of doing future business with the Colombian guy, Peso pocketed the card. Once he took his seat at the table and was about to tell Suave about his encounter with Manuel, Peso was interrupted by Suave mentioning that he was ready to leave.

After footing the bill and leaving a hefty tip for the sexy ass young Colombian waitress, the gang of drug dealers headed towards the exit.

As they emerged from the entrance, there was Cobra, arm-in-arm with his girlfriend Venus, walking towards them. It was like finding a proverbial needle in the haystack, only Suave had not been looking.

"Bitch ass nigga, you a fuckin' traitor," Cobra sneered when he recognized Suave. "You took advantage while I been gone to grab what's rightfully mine."

"You the one who hadn't trusted me enough to get in touch with me and let me know what's up after yo' scary ass ducked off," Suave told him assertively.

"And now you consider yourself runnin' shit, and you boastin' about it on the 'Gram and makin' paper that's mine."

"If you wasn't tryin' so fuckin' hard to duck action from Tito, then you wouldn't have to worry about me runnin' shit now."

"If I'on smoke you right now, it's outta respect for my bitch," Cobra threatened.

It did not take much to make the smaller Suave furious. He marched up to Cobra, who towered over him by a foot. "Nigga, we can shoot it out anytime you want. You name the place," Suave challenged.

"It'll be when you least expect it, so I advise you to stay poled up."

Cobra's girlfriend nervously tugged on her man's arm. Suave's crew pulled him away. Without another word, Cobra and his girl brushed past the small crew and disappeared into the restaurant. Suave nem headed for their ride.

Instead of remaining in Miami one more night to get lit as originally planned, Suave decided he'd rather them drive back to Milwaukee that very night. His two shooters, Rock and another young gun, sat up front while Suave and Peso rode in back of the rented Mercedes-Benz G Wagon. During the drive, Peso tried to reason with Suave.

"I'on give no fuck how Cobra feels. He can try me if he wants," Suave raved. He exhaled a thick cloud of weed smoke.

"Suave, if you hadn't been so fuckin' cocky, you could have settled shit with Cobra right then and there. All it would have taken was a few words of explainin' how he left you in a fucked up position," Peso told him.

Suave scoffed. "Dawg, I'on have to explain myself to dude bitch ass. He's the one with the problem, not me." He hit the blunt, then passed it to Peso.

"Why don't you make a deal with him? You could still work shit out with him," Peso suggested, then puffed the weed.

"Fuck that nigga!" Suave spat. "If Tito's shooters don't get to Cobra first, either he'll kill me, or I'll kill him."

***

Since Suave had ran into Cobra, a few weeks had gone by. Within that timeframe, Cobra had spread the word on social media that Suave's end was imminent. But Suave kept on about his business with a shooter close by at all times. If Cobra wanted some smoke, then Suave wasn't afraid. Although, while Cobra wanted to be in beef with him, Suave just wanted to get money.

It was late in the afternoon and Suave was riding with Rock on the way to check on a load that was to be delivered to his stash house. While Rock steered the Porsche truck, Suave rode in the passenger side. Several blocks from the stash house, Suave saw a car approaching, the driver waving frantically. Both vehicles braked next to one another in the middle of the street. The driver of the car was one of Suave's faithful dope fiends that he served heroin.

"Be careful," the fiend warned. "They're waiting up ahead to kill you. Cobra's crew."

"How do you know?" Suave pressed.

"When I left your spot after copping a fix, a guy with gold teeth had stepped out in front of my car and searched it and mentioned to the others that you wasn't inside the car."

"Where are they?"

"They're in two cars at the end of the block your spot is located on."

"Is Cobra with 'em?" Suave wanted to know eagerly.

"I don't know if he's there too, but I see plenty of guys with guns," the fiend answered.

"Thanks. I'ma be sure to give you a package for the info," Suave promised before sending her along. His blood began to boil. He was not about to duck action. He was gonna pull up and show them what he was made of. Suave reached down to grab the Draco from the floorboard and made sure it was ready for action. "You drive on. I'm gettin' in the backseat," he told Rock.

Grabbing some extra clips, Suave shoved his Glock .40 with a converter switch into the pocket of his jeans and jumped into the backseat of the truck. Rock checked his twin Glock .19s and placed them, chambered and cocked, in his lap. He put the whip in gear and drove towards the stash house. Suave ducked low in the backseat of Porsche truck, ready to hop out at the right moment.

The ambush site was a few blocks away. The side street turned into a one-way street. One had to drive a couple of blocks west to get back on the main street. Cobra's shooters were waiting on both sides, in two separate vehicles. As soon as they knew it was Suave at the corner, they were gonna Swiss cheese his whip.

But the advance warning had allowed Suave to prepare. When Rock drove up onto the corner, the shooters could see only one man, and it was not Suave. They let Rock drive through. Once the Porsche reached the other side of the street, the guy with a mouthful of gold teeth walked into its path with a pistol in hand, causing Rock to brake. Right then, Suave jumped out from the backseat of the truck, firing a burst from his Drac' over the hood of the Porsche at Gold-Mouth.

Boc-boc-boc-boc-boc!

As the man dropped to the ground, Suave turned his fire on the gang of shooters that emerged from the vehicle the moment Gold-Mouth had halted the Porsche. Several of those men fell from the impact of bullets. Rock leaped from the Porsche cab at the same moment, bustin' towards the shooters in the vehicle on the other side of the street. The hammering of machine guns became thunderous. Bullets coming from three directions tore into the Porsche. Rock was popped numerous times and crashed onto the ground. Suave came from beside the Porsche truck and ran up the street bustin' backwards with the Draco.

Gold-Mouth had only been grazed by Suave's initial spray of bullets, and had hugged the ground to play dead and keep out of the line of fire. When he saw Suave running, he got onto his knees and aimed his FN handgun.

Boom-boom-boom-boom!

Three slugs tore into Suave's spine. He fell face forward to the ground. Suave crawled a short distance, scratching and clawing at the ground, writhing in the street. Gold-Mouth jumped in his vehicle and drove over Suave's frail body again and again before finally driving over his head. Suave was already dead when one of the men with a machete went up to the body, raised the blade high in the air, and then brought it down with such force that it cut off the top of Suave's skull at the hairline.

The assailants fled with their own dead and wounded. Only the bodies of Suave and Rock were later found.

**

Several days following the murder, many people had come to Suave's funeral. A small stone church on the city's south side was festooned in black. A priest celebrated a requiem mass in the belief that Suave's charity to the hood absolved at least some of his sins. Then, the pallbearers, one being Peso, emerged from the church with the coffin on their shoulders and carried it through the thick crowd to the hearse. The funeral procession ended at Suave's gravesite, where he was buried.

Subsequent to Suave's funeral, Peso drove on his way home while listening to Fredo Bang's track "2 Death." Once he arrived at his place, he pulled his

Beamer truck to the curb and parked. He then made his way inside the house. His young daughter ran into his arms. He pecked her on the cheek. After hugging her daddy, Maxine took off. Peso turned and entered the master bedroom and sat in edge of the king-sized bed. He was still upset from the funeral. A part of Peso resented Cobra for having his close friend murdered, yet he understood that it was just part of the game.

Mona waltzed into the bedroom to check on him. "I'm sorry about your friend, Lupe," she said as she sat on edge of the bed beside Peso.

"It was tough on me seein' him buried today. Made me realize that I can't be afraid to die," he told her.

"Don't even think like that. You have a lot to live for."

"Mona, only thing I have to live for is you and Max. Nothin' else matters to me."

Mona grabbed his hand in hers and said, "Your dad would want you to live your life."

"Livin' like my dad is why I'm liable to lose my life," Peso responded sullenly. "Look Mona, why don't you give me a moment alone while I clear my head."

Mona understood that Peso needed a moment alone. She kissed him gently on the lips before leaving him to his thoughts.

Peso couldn't help but hold thoughts about Suave. He reflected on something Suave had once said: Bein' the kingpin comes with friends and enemies alike comin' for your crown.

Suave's memory lived on in the heart of his family and friends and in irregularly shaped bone fragments about the size of a quarter that had been cut from the portion of Suave's skull severed by the machete. Holes had been drilled through the fragments allowing thin gold chains to be inserted. The skull-fragment pendants began showing up around the necks of south side dealers, giving grounds for rumor that Cobra remained in charge even though he was rarely seen again on the south side of Milwaukee.

The skull fragments were emblems of loyalty and were grim warnings against betrayal.

CHAPTER 6

The murder of Suave left the drug movement without a capo throughout the city's south side. Raids by the DTF, though not unusual even when someone ran the area, became more frequent and indiscriminate. The raids were the government's way of asserting authority whenever some sensational murder was played up by the media. With Suave dead and gone, those who would normally have been alerted about the coming of cops now somehow did not get the message and would wound up in the back of paddy wagons, handcuffed.

Following Suave's death, the south side underworld expected some arrangement with the DTF to be worked out quickly. Peso knew how risky it was to operate without some sort of patronage. Get caught with drugs and one could expect an harsh interrogation and a long sentence—unless, of course, you had enough cash on hand to pay off the DTF.

At the same time, the market was boomin'. But compared to the days of Suave, however, not that much dope was being made available; it was becoming a drought. Niggas with drugs to sell were being cautious. As weeks dragged on, longtime weight buyers threatened to take their money elsewhere.

Like the other hustlers, Peso moved just enough heroin and marijuana to string along his clientele. He realized that someone was going to have to take over the drug trade if business was to flourish again.

Gathered at Lu's Bar & Grille, some of the most important drug dealers met to decide what to do. Peso was present, along with Raul and Juan, as were two other up-and-coming trappers, Vic and Chop. About a dozen other people involved to one degree or another in drug trafficking were also there. Except Salvador or his two sons, Junior and Ceaser.

The trappers chatted as they stood around having drinks. Almost all of them had drugs that needed to be moved immediately.

"Man, I got pounds of weed that I need to sell in order to pay off the supplier, but I ain't sure if the Drug Task Force will be all over me," Vic said. He had worked as a runner for Cobra, and then for Suave after Cobra disappeared. Like Peso, Vic had become big enough to work his own deals.

Vic was educationally cut above the typical dope boy. Originally from Juarez, México, his mother was a pious woman who went to church faithfully. She prayed fervently that her son would not succumb to worldly temptations and would serve God. Vic's mother's prayers were as focused as a blowtorch, aimed at severing the bonds between Vic and his wayward uncles. In the end, the uncles won the battle over Vic's soul. He abandoned the church to move drugs for his uncles until he started his own drug operation.

"Someone gotta go and make a deal with the DTF," Chop added. He, meanwhile, was a road runner who trafficked loads for anybody who needed his services and was willing to pay his fee.

Chop was mysterious to everyone. He had light skin and thin, fine features, in contrast to the swarthy, rough-hewn men around him. He was quiet and timid seeming. Among his close associates, it was known that Chop and his wife once killed several Mexican Federal Judicial Police in a shootout, who had come to arrest him for drug trafficking. He and his wife were on the run when they fled to the United States. Chop never liked to talk about the shooting. Trafficking drug loads was a way to make a living for Chop.

Vic voiced, "Suave was makin' monthly payments to the captain. If we want to work out a hustle arrangement, that's where we need to start. And Peso, you'd be a good one to do it." Some of the others nodded in agreement.

Peso aspired to be the kingpin. But he knew the DEA was on him so he wanted to lie low. While in charge, Suave had told his friend Peso in general how things were arranged. But Peso was too hot. No, Peso introspectively reasoned, it's better to operate under someone's else's wing—at least for now.

Seated on a bar stool, Peso looked around and said, "Nah, I got all kinds of heat right now."

"What about one of Salvador's sons, Junior or Ceaser?" Juan inquired.

"They didn't even wanna be here without their dad," Peso pointed out.

Salvador was still in federal prison where he ran his drug business from, using his sons to carry out the deals. Yet, Salvador only had several months until he returned to the streets.

"Besides," Chop chimed in, "Ceaser still owes me some paper from a drug deal and haven't paid me back yet. So I rather him not be in charge."

"Then, who can we get?" Vic asked the group.

"Give me a vehicle and I'll drive it. That's all I wanna do," Chop said, making it clear he did not aspire to do anything else.

The field of candidates were pretty slim. Some of the men at the informal gathering weren't at all Mexican. Others were too young, too old, too inexperienced or too unreliable to be seriously considered. Other than Peso, there were only a few possibilities.

"Why don't you go, Vic," Peso suggested.

"How do I know about all this? I've never done it before," Vic protested.

"You know what's goin' on," Peso said. "You hung around with Cobra. You hung around with Suave. You see how it works up and down the ladder."

Raul went through Vic's curriculum vitae: "Plus, you've crossed loads across the border for

Suave and know all of his stash houses; all of your paper is tallied up; you're a smooth talker; you ain't too young; you ain't on nobody's wanted list in México or the States; and you never been to jail."

Peso offered to back him with whatever money was necessary to make the hustle fee payments. "I'll contribute my part and a lil bit more if I have to. I'm sure others here feels the same way." He pointed around the room to various trappers, each nodded in agreement.

"Aight. I'll do it," Vic agreed. "I'll meet with the captain of the DTF."

"Just convince him you know what's goin' on and you're willin' to take over the south side," Peso told him.

Only Chop raised any objections. "I know someone has to do it, but I'on like it. Once you start payin', they'll bleed you for the rest of your life and you can never get out of it," he stressed. Chop knew they were stymied without some sort of arrangement with the DTF. But, he also knew that plain greed made protection costly and precarious.

"Don't worry, Chop. I'll make sure to set shit straight with the captain," Vic responded, sure of himself.

***

Cartel Money

A few days following the meeting at Lu's, Vic got in touch with the captain through another dirty cop. He was forced to cool his heels for several days before being allowed to see Captain Danielson. Not that Danielson refused to see him, he was just hardly available. After some waiting, Vic was finally contacted and directed to show up at an abandoned warehouse, alone.

Before going to the warehouse, Vic had thoroughly gone over what he would say with Peso and Chop and with anyone else with an interest in his success. They knew that the captain had his informants and probably already had at least a general idea of who was doing what on the south side, so there was no use hiding everything from him. On the other hand, there was no use telling him everything, either.

Vic pulled up to the warehouse, a garage door was lifted and he drove his black Infiniti Q60 into the building. There were a few tough-looking men armed with guns present. Vic stepped out of the SUV and was immediately frisked by one of the men. Another one shoved Vic towards an adjacent room. Once he entered, it was a small, unremarkable room except for the machine guns stacked in the corner. The captain didn't bother to get up from the chair he was seated in. He looked Vic up and down and motioned to a chair.

"Talk," Captain Danielson commanded, eyeing Vic intensely.

"'Preciate you giving me your time, Captain. I'm sure you're a very busy man. I'on mean to bother you, but this meeting is necessary, Captain." Vic punctuated his sentences with "Captain" to show his respect.

"Go on," the captain urged, trying to have Vic finally get around to the real purpose of the meeting.

"We can't move much product because nobody has immunity, Captain. I want your blessing to work the south side," he laid out.

"How do you know that I'm the person to come to for this sort of thing?"

"Well, I worked for Cobra for some time. I worked for Suave. I know what's goin' on."

The captain kept pressing him about why he had come to him for this request. "How do you know to come to me?"

"I sometimes drove Cobra to meet with you to bring the hustle fee."

The DTF captain drilled him a while longer, then ended the interview by standing up and walking to the door. He motioned for someone to come, and soon two of the tough-looking goons Vic had seen standing around appeared in the doorway. Captain Danielson pointed at Vic and said, "Get him ready for me."

Vic would soon wish he stuck with the priesthood. The blue goons led him from the room to another room in the back where they strapped him onto a chair and threw a hood over his head. They began beating him. Between the punches came questions.

"Who are you really?" Danielson demanded to know.

"I was a worker for Cobra. I moved loads. What more can I tell you?" Vic pleaded.

The beating was all the more terrifying because Vic was blinded and never knew when or where the next blow would fall. The beatings lasted on and off for some hours. They rammed Vic's head into a bucket of water until he thought he was going to drown; they strapped him naked to a bench and jabbed his thighs and testicles with a cattle prod, sending jolts of electricity through him; and then came the punches. The incessant punches to the rib cage, the abdomen, the kidneys and the head.

During the severest of the torture, the captain was absent. He came in during the respites, taking the role of friend and protector rather than tormentor, asking questions in almost a fatherly tone. Vic had gone to the warehouse to seek permission to work the south side and instead he found the ultimate confessional. He finally told the DTF captain everything he wanted to know, about himself, about his entourage, about their activities.

Then several hours later, Captain Danielson came into the room Vic was being held. He sat in a chair in front of Vic, eyed him sharply, and said, "I'm satisfied that you have balls."

Sure, Vic had talked, but he had put up resistance, and it took more than usual to break him down. "It's apparent from the interrogation that you have connects and a solid organization. You go ahead and work the south side area, but have ten thousand bucks for me every month. And I want the first payment the day after tomorrow."

***

Bruised and shaken but relieved, Vic went to Lu's the next day. When he entered the Bar & Grille, he saw Peso sitting alone at a table near the back of the place and made his way over.

"Been wondering what happened during the meetin'. What took you so long to come back? And fuck happened to your face?" Peso inquired as Vic took a seat across from him.

"Man, the captain had his fuckin' goons hold my ass captive. They tortured me," Vic informed in a voice strained with fear.

Peso looked puzzled. "Why would he do some shit like that?"

"He pressed me to know about certain things. He wanted to know who my connect is and how much product we can move. He also wanted to know about you and some others."

"What'd you let him know?"

"Just basic shit. I'm tellin' you Peso, those sons of bitches ain't human. Thought they were gonna kill me. But we got permission," Vic told him.

It took a while for Vic to get over the torture. He was a healthy thirty-year-old with lots of bitches. He tried not to complain about the lingering pain from the electric shocks, but did confide to close friends that he thought he had been permanently damaged. For the next six weeks, he just couldn't get hard.

CHAPTER 7

Juan upped his Glock .17 equipped with a fifty-shot drum and converter switch, then aimed it at Raul, who pushed the deadly weapon's barrel away. He and Juan liked to draw on each other for practice.

Juan chuckled. "See, you coulda been dead!"

"You got me on that one, Juan. Don't think it's gonna always be sweet like that with opps," Raul reminded him.

Juan stuffed the blick on his waist, and said, "One day, I'm certain, a fast draw will make a crucial difference between my life and a opp's."

"Just make sure he not a opp, he just another victim."

Peso piped in. "Aye, will you two niggas quit goofin' around and help count up this paper."

In the back office of Lu's Bar & Grille, Peso and the others were calculating funds that had been collected from the trap spots. Thus far, they had counted upwards to sixty Gs, and still had more to add up. While they were in the office handling the cash, some shooters were in front of the establishment, watching over things like a hawk.

Juan wrapped a rubber band around a stack of bills. "How much paper do you think we made?" he asked, referring to the profits they were counting up.

"Nothin' compared to what we was makin' when Suave was in charge of shit," Peso admitted. "Now that Vic's the one in charge, at least we make some good money."

"Word on the street is Salvador and his sons don't honor Vic runnin' things," Raul mentioned. "Salvador just wanna be the one in charge instead."

"Well, Salvador need to honor the fact that he's not, or there will be some problems whenever he get outta the feds," Juan added.

"One thing's fa sho, if I was the nigga in charge, then everyone would know it's death before dishonor," Peso declared. He knew that once Salvador was back in the streets there was bound to be a power struggle.

While the trio counted up profits, Peso fed bills into the money counter, Juan wrapped stacks of cash with rubber bands, and Raul tossed each of the stacks inside of a red Gucci tote bag. Afterwards, they would take the paper to the stash house.

Once Peso's iPhone began to ring, he answered the call on speakerphone as he continued his task. "Talk to me."

"I got that cheese that I owe you. Pull up on me and scoop it up," the caller, Greedy, said. He had been given some H on front.

"I'll be there in a sec."

"Cool. So check it out, we been dealin' with each other for a lil while now, and I make sure you get your bread every time you hit my hand. Why don't you hit me with a whole one this time around? That way we both make more money," Greedy pitched.

Peso briefly gave it some thought. "Aight. I'll get it to you later." He ended the call with plans to deliver Greedy a brick of boy.

"Peso," Juan began, "Are you sure about frontin' dawg with that much work?"

"Maybe you shouldn't front him a brick," Raul suggested.

"Greedy brings in good money," Peso reasoned.

Raul shook his head and input, "All money ain't good money."

"He's been payin' up, so this is just an opportunity to get paid more," Peso explained. "Either that, or I'll get paid in blood."

"Say no more," Juan responded, thirsty for blood.

After counting up all of the cash, Peso had Raul and Juan along with him on the way to the stash house. They were in Raul's Range Rover with him gripping the steering wheel, Juan in the passenger side and Peso in the backseat. While dropping off the money, Peso would pick up the key of boy that needed to be delivered.

Once they was near the stash house, Raul spun around the block twice just to be sure that no one was tailing them. After the Range slid to the curb and parked in front of the stash house, Raul and Juan kept their eyes peeled for anything amiss as Peso stepped out with the tote bag in one hand and his fonickle in the other and made his way inside. He stashed away the money in the floorboard of the closet, then collected the brick of dawg food before leaving out. When he returned to the Range, then they were on the way to drop off the product, riding to Finesse2Tymes's track "Rules To The Streets."

Arriving at the H spot on 6th & Beecher Street, Raul veered the Range to the curb and kept a foot on the brake. It being night out, the red brake lights glared. Observing the rundown house from behind the tinted windows, the trio observed there were two niggas posted on the front porch both clutching the poles on their waists while intensely eyeing the Range Rover.

Peso checked to be sure his switch was cocked. "I'ma talk with Greedy. Y'all just be on point," he instructed and sat the weapon on his lap. He grabbed his iPhone and texted Greedy to come outside.

"Every time we pull up on this nigga I get a bad vibe," Juan pointed out. He had his hand rested on the AR-15 in his lap.

"So do I," Raul seconded as he pulled twin Glocks from beneath his seat.

"I'ma make this shit quick," Peso said as Greedy emerged from the spot and approached the Range.

Greedy was a stout, tall, high-yellow complexed nigga with freckles and long dreadlocks and had his four top front teeth gold. He ran a small gang that moved heroin. Dumpin' work was his thing, but Greedy kept shooters on deck.

Pulling open the backdoor, Greedy climbed into the backseat beside Peso. He couldn't help but notice the big .45 in Peso's lap, along with Raul's and Juan's weapons on display. Greedy was poled up himself. Such was the way in the streets.

"Here's what I owe you," Greedy said as he handed over a knot.

Peso unrolled the knot of cash. "Good lookin'." He counted it. Once the numbers added up, he pulled out the brick and warned, "Greedy, make sure I get paid."

"Don't I always," was Greedy's response as he accepted the kilo.

Once Greedy stepped outta the Range, Peso nem pulled off. One way or another, Peso wanted to be paid in full.

***

Entering the Hyatt hotel, Peso found his way up to its lobby bar. He had gone there alone to meet with Manuel, the Colombian man from Miami, pertaining to potential business. Since meeting him, Peso had talked with him via phone a few times to discuss some things. But there were certain things

Manuel was just against discussing over the phone for precautionary measures, so he decided it would be best that he take a flight to Milwaukee in order to work out the details in person with Peso. Plus, he wanted to see for himself the potential of the city.

Turns out that Manuel was part of a powerful group of Colombian traffickers who were responsible for producing sixty percent of the cocaine consumed in the United States. Miami was the control center of trafficking operations in the States for all the big-name Colombian traffickers. As it became costly to do business through Florida, however, the Colombian dealers began to seek out promisingly smuggling organizations throughout the U.S. to flood with product.

When Peso took notice to the well-dressed man, who was sitting alone, he joined Manuel, taking a seat across the table from him.

"Care for a drink?" Manuel offered, handling a glass of Scotch.

"A double shot of Casamigo will do," Peso requested. Waving over a waiter, Manuel placed the order, and then sent him away. "So," he began, returning his attention to Peso, "Let's talk." He took a swig from his glass.

"Let's."

Manuel took a swig from his glass. "I want to move kilos of cocaine through your operation here."

"How many keys are you talkin', and at what cost to me?" Peso inquired with interest.

"I'm talking about twenty kilos to start; and at ten grand each. If all goes well, then we can renegotiate the quantity and cost."

Peso liked the sound of the deal. "Let's say that I'm willin' to take you up on your offer, how soon can I expect the product?" The waiter returned and delivered Peso his drink, then vanished. Peso took a shot of the Tequila.

"As soon as my next shipment arrives from Colombia, I'll have the load prepared for you." Manuel discretely passed Peso a sample of the cocaine. "That, my friend, is pure. Are you in, or not?"

Peso examined the coke, then tooted some of it and immediately felt its effect. "I'm in."

Manuel leaned back in his seat. "Then, you'll be responsible for ensuring that I am paid for the load. One of my couriers will bring it directly to you here in Milwaukee," he laid out. "By the way, this is a nice little town."

"It's no Miami, but this town made me."

"I don't doubt it." Manuel smirked. He raised his glass. "To us making more money."

Peso understood that the deal with Manuel would produce more money. However, that was bound to breed more problems from the opps and from the alphabet boys.

CHAPTER 8

With the hustle fee arrangement in place, Vic slept soundly at night, free of fear of arrest, at least from the DTF.

While Vic was in charge, the south side was relatively peaceful, a reflection of Vic's character and the fact that business was thriving. There was a share for everyone, so why beef? Enforcement was discreet. It usually consisted of pistol-whipping someone who had not paid debts. One way or another, miscreants who did not pay their bills were made to cough up.

Ordinary citizens knew drugs were moving through their neighborhood, but it was a quiet, low-key activity, and people went about their day-to-day lives without giving it much thought. The drug dealers did their thing. The residents did theirs.

It was evening when Captain Danielson showed up at Vic's crib. He left his goons in the vehicle while he walked into the house without even knocking.

Vic and several of his boys lived in a large brick house with a king-sized bed in each of the four bedrooms, a PlayStation and 75" flat-screen TV in the front room, and a well-stocked kitchen and bar. The house was an oasis of luxury in an unremarkable neighborhood near Lu's Bar & Grille.

Peso avoided Vic's place most times in case the captain dropped by, and with good reason. The arrangement with Danielson had its downside.

When the captain entered unannounced, he found Vic and one of his boys, Eddy, seated on the white leather couch in the front room. Danielson strode inside and spotted a chrome-plated .9 semiautomatic pistol with a pearl handle lying on the end table.

"What a little beauty," Danielson commented as he picked up the pistol. He stuffed it on his waist and looked around for something else to take. The captain had a habit of commandeering anything that was not nailed down. He then looked to Vic, and said, "How're things going?"

"Things are goin' good, Captain," Vic answered shakily.

"Good." Danielson's attitude had changed remarkably since that first day in the warehouse. Once grim inquisitor, he was now Vic's compadre. Captain plopped down on the couch beside Vic. "Why don't you get me a drink."

As Vic stepped over to the bar to make him a drink, the captain sent Eddy to fetch his own men from outside. Those blue goons, some of the very ones who had participated in Vic's torture, made themselves comfortable on one of the couches and asked for drinks too. After Vic served up the drinks, he returned to the couch beside the captain, who he was somewhat intimidated by. Danielson was ready to get down to his real purpose of being there.

Cartel Money

"I hate to have to show up at your place with some bad news," Danielson began. "It's gonna cost you more to hustle. Ten grand was okay for starters, but I'm getting a lot of pressure from higher up. A lot of heat's coming down, so I have to put higher fees on you to let you guys move product. I need twenty thousand a month from now on."

"But we're not movin' as much product as you think," Vic argued, but it didn't matter.

"Bullshit! My informants told me how much you and your crew are moving. Now, either you cough up twenty large monthly, or I'll be forced to do my job, Vic."

Vic was stuck in between a rock and a hard place. Just as Chop had predicted in the meeting at Lu's, the captain soon grew greedier and put pressure on Vic for more money. What the crooked cop wanted, the crooked cop got. After all, he had the federal police and the office of the Attorney General behind him and, if necessary, the army.

***

A couple of weeks later, a meeting was called by Vic and everyone gathered at Lu's. At the hike of the hustle fee, Vic had to pass the word on to Peso, to Chop and to everyone else pitching in in pretty much the same language Captain Danielson had used. Vic did not want to, but he had to in order to explain the raids lately.

The dealers stood around awaiting Vic to speak. It being after hours Lu's was closed so they had the place to themselves.

Stepping in front of the crowd of men, Vic got their undivided attention. "Listen up," he began. "I know for a moment we all been able to move work without any heat. But lately, twelve has been in our business."

"What's up with that shit, Vic? If we have an arrangement with the DTF, then there's no way they should be raidin' our spots so much," Juan voiced and others.

Vic looked into the faces before him. "I hate to be the bearer of bad news, but what's up is the captain came to me and told me that his superiors has been on his case so he has to raise the fee to twenty Gs monthly if he's gonna allow us to hustle. And if he doesn't receive it, then he'll have to do his job," he explained.

"I tried warnin' y'all that this shit would happen," Chop chimed in heatedly. "This is just the captain's way of bleedin' you for more money."

"The only way to put an end to the raids is to come up with the payments. So, we all gotta pitch in some more if we wanna keep dumpin' without worryin' about the DTF on top of others," Vic tried to reason.

"And then, that crooked ass muthafuckin' pig is just gonna hike up the fee again. We shouldn't pay up shit," Chop protested and some others agreed.

"Nah, we'll pay the fee," Peso piped in. "With how much paper we're makin', as a unit that fee won't hurt our pockets. But all of the raids damn sure will. So, let's put a stop to it before it gets unbearable."

Even though Peso did not care to pay the greedy crooked cop, he realized what was at stake for all of them. None of them could afford major drug busts or to be arrested. Thereof paying off Captain Danielson would prevent either circumstance. One thing for sure, Peso wanted to set things straight with the captain.

Once the meeting was adjourned, Vic sought out Peso, who was talking with some of the other dumpers. He pulled Peso aside for privacy.

"Good lookin' for helpin' me keep shit in order," Vic told him. "Seems like a lot if niggas don't think I should have this position, especially Junior and Ceaser and their dad. But fuck 'em."

"Yeah, I heard word on the street that Salvador and his sons weren't honorin' you bein' in charge," Peso admitted.

"Word is most want you to be in charge, Peso. And I personally don't disagree."

"But, Vic, you the one in charge instead, and I honor that. Just watch your back 'cause if someone like Salvador wants your spot bad enough, then he'll come for it one way or another," Peso expressed. "Even still, don't let nothin' stop you from focusin' on makin' money moves."

Vic nodded his understanding. "Fa sho. Speakin' of, I got a money move that I'm finna put down in Las Vegas. How 'bout you fly out there with me in a few days to oversee that the deal goes good. Plus, afterwards we can kick it there for a few days."

"My boy, I'd like to but I got too much shit here goin' on at the moment to take that trip with you."

"Maybe next time," Vic suggested. "Listen, I hate that this is happenin' with the captain but, what can I do? Thanks for understandin' my position."

"Vic, I'm just tryin' to make sure we can all keep gettin' money without twelve in our way," Peso told him. "And, if I was in charge, what I would do is make the crooked cop understand he works for me, I don't work for him." He wanted Vic to know what it takes to be the head nigga in charge.

"Understood," Vic replied.

Over time, Vic ended up paying twenty-five grand a month. It was tough, but at least the raids by the DTF had come to a halt.

***

Vic had a shipment of a half-ton of marijuana en route by road to Las Vegas. As a precaution, he wanted to oversee the shipment. He rarely traveled with loads, but this time he wanted to supervise the deal himself. It was the first time he was distributing that far west, and he wanted to make sure nothing went wrong. In addition, he had always had an itch to see how the famed Sin City of the desert was.

Vic had Eddy along with him being that Peso opted out of the trip. They were waiting in Mitchel International Airport to board their Las Vegas flight. It was early in the morning and they were scheduled to reach their destination around noon.

"The others are drivin' the load to Vegas as we speak. Once we arrive there, then we'll meet them at the hotel," Vic laid out.

"Vic, we don't even know the guy well that you're gonna deal with. What if he plans to finesse you or rob you?" Eddy asked.

"That's exactly why there's also some artillery comin' along in the car with the load. Ain't no way in hell am I goin' into this deal without a blick on me," Vic assured. "Now just chill. I got everything under control. We'll take care of the deal, then hit up some casinos to some gamblin'. And we'll be back home in three days tops."

"Say no more."

Once it was time to board their flight, Vic and Eddy headed towards the gate. Suddenly, federal agents appeared six deep and nabbed them.

"Hell is this about?" Vic asked as he was being handcuffed.

"Victor Avila," the agent cuffing him said sternly. "You are under arrest for drug trafficking, money laundering, tax evasion and other charges."

The DEA had in hand an arrest warrant based on a secret nineteen-count indictment that had been handed down by a federal grand jury in Milwaukee three months earlier. Vic did not have an inkling of the indictment until the arrest at the airport.

CHAPTER 9

Over time Ambrose, Cobra, Suave, Vic and other drug dealers transformed the south side into a bigger narcotics hub than had ever before existed in the city. Large seizures of heroin and marijuana distributed from there were now being made throughout the state. Intelligence from narcotics seizures showed that those drugs had been smuggled into the United States from México.

After Vic's arrest, Peso took over the south side. He had his own couriers and his own sources of heroin and marijuana in the interior of México. During the time Vic was running the scene, Peso very coolly and methodically cultivated the right people, placing himself into position to rise to power when the moment arrived. And he was not at all subjected to the same gauntlet of interrogations that Vic had undergone in the warehouse. Whoever worked for Vic or had benefited from his hustle arrangement with the captain of the DTF had switched loyalty to Peso. Now, Peso was paying the hustle fee and was the one in charge of Milwaukee's south side drug trade.

While accompanied by some of his boys, along with Sierra, Peso attended a car show that was held at Longfellow Park. It was easy to identify the drug bosses. Majority of them had semiautomatics equipped with sticks protruding from their waistbands while some of the more important ones, like Peso, wore bulletproof vests and had some shooters walking in step with them.

The drug bosses had some of the most expensive vehicles there on display. There were many vehicles of all types and models and years presented at the event. Peso also had his own BMW 760 that was royal blue and embellished with chrome 24-inch Rucci rims on display.

Peso and the others walked around admiring vehicles. He stopped to interact with some people that he knew whenever they crossed paths. Now that he was runnin' shit everybody who was somebody knew it, including the Drug Enforcement Agency.

The DEA was not surprised when informants began relating the chain of command. Peso, they were told, had taken over the south side. Peso's name had begun to figure more and more prominently in the DEA intelligence reports. Increasingly, drug dealers snatched up throughout the city named Peso as their plug.

There was an agent about twenty yards from the drug boss, pretending to admire some vehicles. When he got the chance, the narc coolly snapped off two frames on his cellphone, photographing Peso. Peso and his boys were none the wiser.

During the tour of the car show, Peso happened to run across a trusted acquaintance named Donnie who was with his wifey, Toya. When Donnie had gotten out of prison, while looking for a job, he met

Peso at Lu's. Peso hired him on as a dishwasher. One night they had a few drinks and it didn't take either long to understand the other's secret occupation. On the side, Donnie and his wifey sold weed out of their house. Peso became Donnie's main weed connect. With a round, blemished face, Donnie was friendly, cool, and amusing. People tended to like him immediately.

"Didn't expect to catch you here," Peso said.

"Yeah, well, I like whips," Donnie replied. "And this one right here is nice as hell!" It was a Ferrari.

"That one is nice," Peso agreed. "Since you here, I wanna talk with you."

"I'm listenin'."

Peso hung an arm around Donnie's shoulder and said, "Bein' you already been coppin' weed from me and doin' odd jobs for me, how 'bout you officially join my crew. You can be one of my runners." He had Chop as a runner, although he knew Donnie was also reliable.

Donnie knew there was good money in trafficking drugs, he had been paid a hefty fee before by Peso to run loads. He replied, "I'll do it. But not only would you have to pay me, but you'd also have to provide me all the vehicles, then I'll make as many runs as you need."

"I got you." Peso knew he could trust Donnie with his loads. "I'll be sure to get in touch with you when I'm in need of a runner."

"You can count on me, Peso," Donnie assured.

After parting ways with Donnie, Peso and his entourage made their way over to his parked BMW. There were numerous people admiring the vehicle as they passed by. Raul and Juan stepped away to entertain some bad bitches that were walking by, leaving Peso alone with Sierra.

"Enjoyin' yourself?" Peso asked his date.

"I am. I never seen so many pretty cars before," Sierra said. She held on tight to his arm, and he didn't mind having her as arm candy.

"Believe me, baby, none of these whips are as pretty as you."

"Awww, that's so sweet."

The more Peso had the chance to spend time with Sierra, the more he was feelin' her. He was feelin' that she was a good girl with a bad bitch attitude. Over time, Peso learned that she was a hairstylist, who owned her own hair salon, and she aspired to one day open up a chain of daycares. All she knew about Peso was that he owned Lu's Bar & Grille but had no idea of what else he may be into. Of course Peso loved Mona, but it didn't prevent him from enjoying Sierra.

"How is it to have so many people's admiration?" Sierra inquired.

"It's just a car. And I'on care much for material shit," Peso told her, referring to his Beamer that people were marveling at.

"I don't mean the car. I mean how people admire you, Peso." Sierra leaned back against the BMW. "Since we've been here, so many have gone out of their way to acknowledge you. I can see how they admire everything about you."

Peso studied her with his eyes. "Most want what they admire about others."

"Well, I admire you for you, not whatever you have."

"Good to know." He pulled open the backdoor of the Beamer and uttered, "How 'bout you come show me how much you admire a nigga."

Peso took Sierra by her petite, manicured hand and ushered her into the back seat of the BMW. Its interior was a cream colored leather. While hid behind the tinted windows, Peso sat back and Sierra straddled his lap. They kissed each other greedily, their tongues danced. Peso palmed her plump ass while she ground her hips. Sierra helped him out of his bulletproof vest, then carefully removed the .45 from his waist and she placed it on the seat beside them. He tugged his Amiri jogger pants down around his thighs and freed his throbbing dick. He pulled her fitted Fashion Nova dress up over her ass to her slim waist, she wore no panties. Sierra grabbed his hardness, then guided it into to her slit, causing her to gasp as she slid down on each inch of his full length.

"Damn girl, this shit so wet," Peso groaned as she rocked back and forth on his dick. He grasped her ass and pounced her up and down on his pipe, causing her to grow wetter between her legs. The feel of her slippery pussy hugging his dick was amazing to him. "You got a nigga dick feelin' so fuckin' good, boo!"

"Oooh... Your dick is all up in this kitty," Sierra moaned in pleasure. She tossed her head back as he lifted her up to the tip of his piece and slammed her down onto its base. "Yaaas, do it just like that." Her wetness felt so damn delightful while he was deep in her.

Sierra kissed Peso while she rode his dick. Their kisses grew passionate. He licked and sucked on her neck, taking in the aroma of her Chanel perfume. The feeling of his full lips all over her caused her to moan softly. Her moans grew louder as she became closer to reaching climax. Peso enjoyed her fuck faces. They were so sexy and turned him on even more. He could feel himself about to bust a nut. His dick was so hard and her pussy was very wet.

"Oh, shit... I'm cummmin!" Sierra purred as an orgasm took control of her mind, body and soul. Her juices oozed and she convulsed. When she creamed all over his dick, Peso was seconds away from bustin'.

"Boo, you about to make a nigga bust," Peso grunted.

She climbed off his lap and took his large dick into her mouth. Sierra stroked his dick with a hand and hungrily sucked its tender tip. Before long, Peso released his semen and she tasted every drop of him.

Afterwards, the two sat in the backseat of the foreign whip half naked, trying to catch their breaths. They could see Raul and Juan standing in front of the BMW while talking with the bad bitches they had stopped. Peso and Sierra began fixing their clothes.

"I really enjoyed that, lil baby," Peso said as he pulled on his vest. He grabbed his .45 and replaced it on his waist.

"So did I," Sierra replied. She fixed her dress. "Peso, why do you have that gun and vest on you?"

Peso looked to her and told her, " Because some will even kill for what they admire."

CHAPTER 10

At the stash house, Peso was meeting with Chop. They were seated on the tan leather couch in the living room while smoking a blunt of Za as Carlito's Way displayed on the huge flat screen TV. Peso had texted him earlier about wanting to discuss business and Chop agreed to meet with him.

Chop was Peso's go to guy when it came to having to deliver major loads. He would smuggle anything, as long as the fee was proper. Over time, he had ran numerous shipments for Peso without a hitch. Therefore, Peso relied upon him to get the job done whenever he needed him.

"Chop," Peso began, "I need three loads of smoke drove to Green Bay in a single night, and I want you to do it for me."

"Give me the details," Chop requested.

"The loads are to be driven to an isolated farm. I need you to get them there tonight, so you'll have to make three round trips. I'll have a crew waitin' for you with a van. And, of course, I'll pay you properly. Three racks each trip."

"I can do that. I'll be back to see you later on. Right now, I gotta go and holla at a couple dudes about some paper they still owe me."

"Need me to send some shooters with you?"

88

"No, I'll be aight by myself. Just some dudes who been puttin' me off for a while. One of 'em is Ceaser," Chop told him.

"Ceaser still owe you? Well I'on see why he wouldn't pay up," Peso said, giving the benefit of doubt. "Just go and handle your business, then get back with me later."

***

About 9:30 at night, Chop took off with the first of Peso's loads. Waiting for him at the Green Bay farm was a crew that included one of Peso's close homeboys, Price, who was in charge of the crew. They had a van there also, just as Peso said it would be, in order to transfer the load from Chop's vehicle, then Chop could set off for the second load of three.

Soon as Chop pulled up and parked, Price's crew began to unload the bales of marijuana and putting them into the van. Chop stepped out of his vehicle to speak with Price concerning the next load. Suddenly, the police moved in several vehicles deep, catching Chop and the others by surprise. DEA had been hiding near the farm, waiting for Chop to arrive.

"DEA!" one of the agents shouted while brandishing his service weapon.

Chop panicked and reached for his pistol.

Boc-boc-boc-boc-boc!

Once Chop went for his weapon, he was shot by the agent in his head and chest. He was not the only casualty. One of the crew members was shot when he aimed a machine gun at the agents. In all, six men were arrested, including Price.

Back in Milwaukee, Peso kept waiting, but Chop never returned for the second load of weed. A few hours after the runner was due back, Peso knew for sure that something had gone wrong. He tried calling Chop and Price's phone only to get no answer. Finally, Peso got a call from one of the crew members.

"Hell's goin' on?" Peso wanted to know.

"There's been a bust. I was the only one to escape," he reported.

Peso straight sat up on the couch. "What happened?"

The man filled Peso in on the details of the drug bust. Afterwards, Peso made a call to Chop's wife to let her know what had happened to Chop during the raid. Slowly details began pouring in.

Peso fell back into the couch with his mind racing. The bust was a serious setback for him. In one night, he lost a runner, some of his crew, a load of marijuana, and one of his close homeboys. Peso was furious. The DEA must have had an advance notice that the load was coming. Now, Peso realized he had to be cautious.

***

"Still can't get over what happened to Chop and Price," Peso vented.

Peso, Raul and Juan were in traffic on the way to the club. It was Juan's idea to take Peso out for the night in order to get his mind off of things. They were riding in Juan's red Infiniti QX60, swervin' through traffic with a car full of shooters behind them. Fredo Bang's track "Federal Raid" played in the background.

"That just goes to show you that we gotta be cautious about who we fuck with," Raul prompted.

Juan dipped around a vehicle. "What we need to do is slide on snitch ass niggas," he added.

"But we don't know for sure who snitched. For all we know, twelve could've gotten lucky with the bust," Peso reasoned. He had his suspicions of who may have tipped off the feds but he wasn't for certain.

Juan scoffed. "Yeah, whatever." He wasn't tryin' to hear that shit. "On some other shit, what you wanna do about Salvador now that his ass is home from the feds?"

"Me and him are gonna have to gain some type of understandin'."

"Peso," Raul piped in, "One thing's for sure, Salvador's only understandin' is that he should be in charge. Just look at how he and his sons didn't honor Vic."

Peso stated, "Unlike Vic, I ain't acceptin' dishonor." He meant that by any means necessary.

Peso realized that Salvador and his sons were going to be a problem sooner or later. However, if need be, he would solve that problem.

"Just remember somethin' our dad used to always tell us," Juan began. "Always look after your hermano'. So trust me, I'll drill or be drilled for you, Peso."

"So will I," Raul seconded.

"And, on dad's grave, I'll do the same for y'all," Peso swore.

Near the destination, Juan swung a turn onto the street that the club was located. Of the three, Juan was more of the clubbing type, so he was ecstatic when he saw how lit the place seemed to be on this night. Peso didn't mind going out to clubs here and there, but Raul was not really a clubber. Somehow, Juan had convinced them to come along for a night of fun. He parked the Infiniti truck in the lot and the car full of shooters parked beside the SUV.

"Let's go inside, pop some bottles, holla at some baddies, and try to get our minds off everything else for the night at least," Juan asked of the two.

Peso, Raul, Juan and the rest of the entourage entered the club, leaving a couple of shooters to chill in the parking lot. The place was occupied by bad bitches who were either chasing after, or being chased by some of the dope boys in the building. Peso and his boys bought their way into VIP where the occupied a table and ordered bottle service. Peso came across some dumpers that he knew from servin' them weight.

Greedy was amongst them. He sent over a bottle of Ace Of Spade to Peso's table. It was apparent to Peso that Greedy had gotten his paper up, judging by the bust-down Cuban link necklace Greedy rocked. He was making plenty money off the brick of boy Peso had fronted him. Now all Greedy had to do was make sure Peso was paid his proper chop. The club was lit and those in attendance were having a grand time. Although, Peso still had other shit on his mental. Fuck the club, he'd rather be countin' money.

***

In the basement of his home, Salvador was discussing matters with his two sons, Junior and Ceaser. The basement area was set up similar to a sports bar; there was a huge flat screen TV mounted on the red brick wall in front of a black leather wraparound sectional, a pool table, a few pinball machines, and a well-stocked bar. Not to mention the collection of guns on display inside of a glass shelf.

After spending nearly two years in federal prison, Salvador was back in the streets with a vengeance. He was making connections while in prison, some of Salvador's jail mates were friends or relatives of important marijuana and heroin distributors in México. These jailhouse contacts arranged introductions after he was soon released, and Salvador's craftiness took care of the rest. Now, he was smuggling drugs heavily out of México, using his newfound connections as his source.

At the same time, rumors were spreading on the south side that Peso and Salvador factions were on a collision course. After Vic had gotten the south side, the word was that Salvador and his sons were not honoring it. That did not change when Salvador got out of federal prison. Salvador apparently had some sort of arrangement of his own with the DTF captain that allowed him to hustle without much interference. Salvador wanted to eventually take over the south side. But Peso had gotten it instead. However, Salvador was eager to be in charge.

"Sons," Salvador opened. He was perched back against the pool table. "Now that I'm out of that hellhole, things are gonna change for better or worse, depending on who's on our side. Since we have our own connects, we don't need anyone else's."

"Pops, what about us at least doin' business with others?" Ceaser inquired as he chalked the pool cue.

"Only way we do any business with others is if we have to. Besides that, we keep our business to ourselves," he explained.

Junior, who was seated on a stool near the bar, said, "How 'bout Peso and his gang? It was one thing when Vic was in charge, but with Peso in charge, I'm sure shit is much tougher."

"Junior, I knew Peso's father, Luis, since before Peso could wipe his own ass. There's no way I'll allow some bastard kid to be this city's Cartel kingpin. If I have to, then I'll make sure Peso goes out just like his father," Salvador declared.

"Like father, like son," Ceaser added with a smirk.

"Peso sent word to me that he wants us to talk in order to gain a mutual understanding. Well, I don't see a need for that. He has his operation to run, and I have mine."

"Maybe our operations can be beneficial to one another's," Junior suggested.

Salvador's took a drink from his glass of tequila. "Maybe. But for now, we'll focus on our own operation and trying to expand it. That said, we have a shipment coming in later today. And I need for you two to go meet with the courier to pick it up."

"We'll take care of it, Pops," said Junior.

"Good."

Martell "T" Bolden

Salvador had his mind made that he was going to eventually be the south side kingpin.

CHAPTER 11

Seated behind the desk inside the office in the back of Lu's Bar & Grille, Peso fed a stack of blue-face hundred-dollar bills into that money machine; it made the 'frrraaap!' sound as it calculated the total sum. He and Raul were counting up the funds accumulated from the latest drug flip. Juan was in the front area of the establishment with some other mafiosos watching the place.

"Here's about thirty bands. Once we count up the rest, we'll put it towards the re-up," Peso said.

"About that, now that Chop is RIP, how're we gon' smuggle the loads from México? He was our go to guy," Raul mentioned. He wrapped a stack of cash with a rubber band.

"I'll talk with Donnie 'bout that. I'm sure he'd be willin' to run our major loads for a proper fee."

"You trust dawg like that?"

"He's never given me a reason not to. Anytime Donnie owed me paper, he paid up," Peso told him. "Speakin' of, that nigga Greedy still owes me some paper, and if he doesn't pay up soon, then I'ma send either you or Juan to drill his ass."

"Enough said," Raul replied coolly. He tossed the stacks of cash into a olive colored leather Dior backpack. "Since you been in charge of shit, we been runnin' up a bag. But I noticed Salvador is still tryin' to make moves without you."

Peso leaned back in his chair. "Sooner or later, me and Salvador ain't gon' have no choice but to talk it out. Or shoot it out." He didn't have any problems with Salvador or his sons as far as he was concerned, but Peso was ready for whatever.

While Peso and Raul were busy counting up the paper-cheese, Juan stepped into the office. "Peso, the chota is here to see you," he said, referring to Captain Danielson.

Send him in, hermano," Peso instructed, not expecting the captain to drop by.

Once Danielson entered the office, Peso offered him a seat. The two men had met before following the arrest of Vic. They had established that now Peso would be the one paying a twenty thousand dollar monthly hustle fee to the captain in order to operate his drug ring without issues with the Drug Task Force. And Peso had made it clear with Danielson that their deal was nonnegotiable.

"Nice establishment you have here," Captain Danielson said. He knew that the place was merely a front for the drug lord to conduct illicit business out of.

Peso rested his elbows atop the desk. "Thanks. But I'm sure that's not why you're here. Wasn't expectin' to see you again until next month." He grabbed a couple stacks of the cash, then tossed across the desk towards Danielson and said, "Twenty Gs."

"'Preciate it." Danielson picked up the stacks and thumbed through it. He continued on, "But I'm not here about the monthly payment."

"Then, what're you here about?"

"Peso, I need to seize some narcotics in order to put it on the books and make things look good with the higher ups. It doesn't have to be much, but something will be better than nothing. And I need it soon," the captain explained.

Peso figured it would be worth offering up a small amount of product in comparison to the large amount he was moving freely. He leaned back in his seat and said, "I'll tell you what, Danielson, there will be a load waitin' for you in one of my spots later on. I'll text you with the location."

The captain made his way out. Though Peso didn't much trust the crooked cop, he would rather use their arrangement to his advantage.

"Raul," Peso started, "Clear out one of the spots and leave a half brick there."

***

Mona was ringing up her final customer before closing time. Like every night, she closed the doors of First Lady Boutique at nine PM sharp. At the boutique, Mona sold women and girl apparel and footwear, along with other womanly accessories and items.

After showing the customer out, just as Mona was finna lock the door, Peso veered his BMW truck to the curb in front of the entrance. He was there to pick up his girl. Peso stepped out of his whip and made his way inside of the boutique. He sat in one of the comfy chairs while she finished up her duties.

"It's been a long, tiresome day," Mona sighed. "I've been on my feet all damn day and they are killing me."

Peso patted his lap and said, "Why don't you come and take a seat and get off your pretty lil feet for a moment."

"Maybe that's a great idea." She tottered her way over to Peso and let out a sigh of relief as she sat in his lap. Peso removed the red-bottom Louis Vuitton stilettos she wore, exposing her small, pedicured feet.

"Now, don't that feel better," he uttered as he massaged her feet.

"Mmmm... Papi, that feels amazing." Mona relaxed while enjoying her feet being caressed. "Lupe, I really want for you to know that I love having you in me and Maxine's lives. But it seems that lately we haven't seen much of you."

"Listen Mona," Peso began in a mellow tone. "I'm out in the trenches everyday dodgin' bullets and cases just to take good care of you and Max, because that's how much I love y'all. So whenever I do have time with my girls, I cherish it. Believe me, I care to spend as much time with you and our daughter as I can."

"And Max and I appreciate what you do for us."

Peso genuinely loved Mona and undoubtedly loved Maxine. Over the years he had been with Mona, he stepped out on her several times before. Although he never left her, more so on the strength of him having a child with her, and Mona knew how to play her position. Even when she suspected him of cheating, she never really complained. Peso treated Mona with respect and treated Max like a princess. He would always make sure they were taken care of.

"Let's go and pick up Max from your mother's house," Mona suggested. As she went to climb out of Peso's lap, he stopped her.

"How 'bout we give 'em a lil more time together," Peso told her, then pulled her mouth onto his and they kissed.

With both of his hands, Peso caressed Mona's pleasant body. She enjoyed the feel of his hands all over her, rubbing her perky breasts, hips and thighs. The two stood to their feet, then Peso tugged Mona's skinny jeans down around her ankles and positioned her bent over the arm of the chair. He knelt behind her, using his fingers to spread her pussy lips, then began eating Mona's pussy from the back.

"Mami, this pussy tastes so damn good," Peso groaned. He sucked her pearl tongue and caused her to buckle at the knees. As his long, thick tongue darted back and forth in the twat, Mona felt bliss.

"Ooooh, shit..." Mona whimpered in pleasure. "Eat it just like that." She enjoyed the feeling of Peso's tongue encircling her slit. Peso tongue-kissed her cleanly shaven pussy with passion. He delighted the taste of her creamy juices as the pussy grew wetter with each pleasurable moment. "Make me cum, papi... Make me cummm," she moaned. It was not long before she came and Peso began slurping her juices.

Rising to his full height, Peso pulled his Palm Angel jeans down, freeing his hard dick. He slid his pipe inside of her satiny love tunnel from behind. "Damn, this shit so warm and tight," he expressed as each inch of his dick filled her. He began fuckin' her from the back and Mona arched her back allowing him a better angle at her wet shot. She threw the pussy back on all of his dick and he gripped her slim waist tight to keep her ass steady. "You like that dick, boo, don't you."

Mona tossed her head back as she took the dick. "Oooh... Mmm, yaaas... Papi. I like this dick so, so much!" she cried out blissfully. It drove her wild when Peso slipped a thumb in her asshole. She enjoyed the double penetration. When she felt herself inching closer to another orgasm, she looked back at him over her shoulder and demanded, "Fuck me, Papi, fuck me..." Her pussy gushed on his dick.

As their flesh clapped with each thrust, Peso felt a nut arising within in the tip of his hardness. He began beating the pussy up. "This wap about to make a nigga nut," Peso breathed. Some strokes later, he released warm semen, then collapsed forward, leaning against Mona and trying to catch his breath.

After taking a breather, the couple fixed their attire. Mona locked up the boutique while Peso awaited in the Beamer truck. Once she entered the passenger side, he pulled off and they were on their way to pick up their daughter.

When they arrived at Tamera's house, Peso parked the BMW at the curb. He and Mona got out the vehicle, then approached the front door and rang the doorbell. Tamera answered the door and let them inside, leading them into the living room where Maxine was sound asleep on the couch.

"Thank you for picking her up from daycare," Mona said to Tamera.

"Anytime," Tamera replied. "I love spending time with her."

"Hope she wasn't too much trouble."

"Not at all. She was a sweetheart," Tamera assured.

Peso scooped his baby girl up into his arms, being careful not to wake her. "It's late. We should get Max home and into bed," he commented.

"Before you go, Mona, will you grab the bag of clothes off my bed that I bought for her?" Tamera asked and Mona obliged.

"Ma, you didn't have to buy her new clothes. She already have plenty to wear," Peso reasoned.

"Well, now she has more. She's my grandbaby, and I wanted to do something for her. Lupe, you really need to be the dad your daughter needs. She talked about wanting to see her papa all day. Sadly, you know how it feels to lose your dad; Maxi doesn't deserve that," Tamera expressed.

Mona returned with a Macy's bag in hand. After Tamera planted a gentle peck on her granddaughter's cheek, Peso and Mona made their way out of the house with Maxine. While Peso strapped his daughter into the car seat, Mona climbed into the passenger side. Once Peso made sure the baby was secure he found his way around to the driver's side and slid in behind the steering wheel. They pulled off on their way home.

It being night out, Peso had on the Beamer's headlights to help lead the way. Light rain drummed the windshield as the wipers swept side to side with a thud. Payroll Giovanni's track "Provider" played at a modest volume in the background. Peso couldn't help but to think about what his mother had told him as he steered the whip through traffic. He glanced over at Mona; he had love for her but figured they wouldn't always be together. However, on the love of his daughter he would always be there to provide for them. As Peso glanced through the rearview at his daughter, something caught his eye.

The vehicle behind him seemed to be tailing him. Peso grabbed his .45 from beneath his seat and held it in his lap. If the vehicle was tailing him, then Peso would do what he had to in order to protect Mona and Maxine. Once he turned the corner, the suspect vehicle continued going straight ahead and Peso was relieved.

Damn, these streets got a nigga on edge, Peso thought to himself. He replaced his blick beneath the seat while steering towards home. One thing for sure, he never wanted to bring heat to where he lay his head.

CHAPTER 12

Needing the next load smuggled from México, Peso decided to go and see Donnie about it. Ever since having Donnie on his payroll, Peso had been relying on him to run small loads here and there. But now that Chop was no longer available, Peso relied on Donnie to become his most important runner.

The Range Rover veered to the curb and parked. Peso stepped out of its passenger side and Raul from behind the steering wheel. They were going to see Donnie at his apartment. Donnie was aware they were coming, being that he had invited them over when Peso called him earlier about them needing to talk.

Once Peso and Raul was buzzed into the complex, they found their way up to the second floor where Donnie's apartment was located and knocked on its door. The door was answered by Donnie's girlfriend, Toya, who let them inside of the place. Donnie was seated on one of the couches, rollin' Za up in a Backwoods blunt, and offered his company a seat. They copped a squat on the vacant couch.

"What's good with you two?" Donnie greeted them.

"We just tryin' to make a livin'," Peso replied.

"I see you rollin' up a blunt. Shit smells like some gas," Raul said, taking in the strong aroma of the high-grade weed.

"It is some gas. Matter of fact, I got it from Peso, so you know it's some good shit comin' straight from México," Donnie responded.

Peso leaned forward and rested his elbows on his thighs. "That's what I actually came here to talk with you about, homeboy."

"I'm all ears." Donnie sparked a Bic lighter and held the flame under the tip of the blunt. His cheeks got hallow and the blunt end glowed. Toya came and sat next to him.

"I got a load that I need for you to go pick up in México and smuggle it back to me. It's ten bricks of boy and thirty pounds of smoke," he informed. "I know this ain't the kind of runnin' job you're used to but I'm willin' to pay you well for bustin' the move."

"How well?" Donnie was interested in knowing.

"Ten bands."

Donnie leaned back in his seat, puffed the blunt and thought on it a moment. "How 'bout you pay me the ten Gs and throw in two pounds of smoke, then we got a deal," he bargained, then exhaled a thick cloud of weed smoke.

"Deal," Peso agreed.

"When do you need for me to bust this move?"

"In two days, my plug there will have the load ready for me. I'ma provide you a vehicle and send a second one with a shooter in it as protection. I'll pay you half of the cash now, then the other half when the job is done. Plus, you'll get the two pounds when I get the load from you."

"Sounds good to me," Donnie said, satisfied with the deal.

Peso's words to many of his drug runners when they prepared to road run could be vaguely menacing, veiled hints at what he might do to them if they let him down in any way. For Donnie it was a sincere, "Good luck to you."

***

Juan was out collecting profits owed to Peso. He had his young shooter, Perry, along with him. Juan pushed his Infiniti truck towards the third stop of the day. He did not mind collecting from niggas who owed because, if need be, Juan was down to make sure a debt was paid one way or another, which is why Peso sent him.

Arriving at the next stop, Juan parked the SUV. He tucked his .40 Glock in the front pocket of his Off What jeans with its thirty-shot stick protruding; and Perry held a Draco in hand on display. The two stepped out the whip and entered the H spot without even bothering to knock. Juan had come to this particular spot to holla at Greedy since he was the nigga in charge of making sure the product gets moved and the profits are in order.

"Damn nigga, you just gon' barge in this bitch like that," one of the spot workers complained and jumped from the couch onto his feet.

If looks could kill, the worker would be dead from the way Juan looked at him and retorted, "Lil nigga, sit the fuck down before I have my boy lay you down." As if on cue, Perry aimed his Drac' at the worker.

"Hol' up, Juan," Greedy protested. "He's my lil cousin who don't know when to chill. Don't mind him."

"Make sure he chill the fuck out before he end up gettin' burnt." Juan motioned for Perry to rest easy. "On some other shit, where that paper at you owe Peso?"

Greedy looked to his younger cousin, and said, "Spider, grab that money real quick." Once Spider returned with some stacks of cash, he handed it to Perry, who kept a close eye on him with his finger of the trigger. "That's all of it," Greedy assured. "Let Peso know that I'm good for another brick."

"As long as your paper's good, I'm sure Peso won't mind frontin' you another one." Juan turned for the door with Perry in tow.

Once Juan and Perry jumped back into the Infiniti truck, Juan directed his young shooter to put the cash inside of the satchel he had brought with, then they were on the way to collect the next debt. After Juan were to make collections for the day, he would head to the stash house to drop off the paper.

Juan glanced over at his young shooter and said, "That shit was real savage how you upped Drac' on ol' boy back there. You had his ass scared as hell!" He busted out laughing.

"I just wanted to let dawg know who the hell he was fuckin' with. Bet his ass chill out now," Perry remarked coolly.

At only twenty-two, Perry was savage with his. He had grown up around Peso nem on the treacherous south side of the city, so Perry had seen, done and experienced some serious shit at his age. He was a brown skin, tall nigga with hazel eyes and rocked a hi-top fade. Perry was about his paper but overall he was an ambitious shooter.

"At least now Greedy knows what to expect if he ever attempt to play Peso outta any money," Juan pointed out.

Juan and Perry made stops at two more spots and collected some money. Neither stop gave them a problem. Subsequent to making his stops, Juan grabbed his iPhone and texted Peso.

Juan:

OTW to drop off $. Meet me at the stash house.

A moment later, Juan received a reply text.

Peso:

OTW. Luv, big bro.

Cartel Money

Juan was on the expressway shooting towards the stash house located in the outskirts of Milwaukee, approximately twenty minutes away in Oak Creek. He knew that Peso would be satisfied with him collecting the profits. One thing for sure, Juan was always willing to do whatever for Peso, and he knew the feeling was mutual. No matter what, Juan was his brother's keeper. While en route, Juan listened to King Von & Lil Durk's track "Evil Twins."

Shortly thereafter, Juan was pulling up to the stash house. He parked his Infiniti truck behind Peso's BMW truck. Juan grabbed the satchel from the backseat, then he and Perry stepped out of the whip and entered the stash house, where they found Peso and Raul standing in the front room.

"Here's the cheese I collected for the day," Juan said as he sat the satchel atop the coffee table.

Peso grinned. "I take it you didn't have no problems collectin' from niggas," he assumed.

"Damn near had a problem with one of Greedy's workers, and Perry here was ready to solve it. You should have seen how he upped Drac' on the goofy ass lil dude." He chuckled at the thought of how caught off guard Spider looked. "Besides that, Greedy paid up. Now, he wants you to front him another block of dawg food."

"That's cool with me. I'll have you drop it off to him tonight."

"Maybe you should just match whatever he can afford to buy and front him that, instead of a whole thang again," Raul strongly suggested. "That way he only owes so much."

"As long as he pays up, I'm willin' to front him whatever he can handle."

"Don't trip Raul, Greedy ass knows what to expect if he ever finesse Peso outta any cheese," Juan assured.

Peso took a seat on the couch, then said, "Let's count up this cash real quick, 'cause I got other shit to do." He dumped the money out of the satchel onto to the coffee table. The others began assisting him with the count. But what counted the most was loyalty over money.

CHAPTER 13

It was late at night and Lu's was closed. The only ones who still remained in the place was Peso, Raul and Juan. The trio were discussing the meeting Peso had set to have with Salvador's son, Ceaser.

Earlier in the day Peso had received a call from Ceaser, who requested to meet with him in order for them to talk business. Peso was not exactly sure of what business Ceaser had with him, mainly since Peso still had yet to have a sit down with Salvador. He was partially skeptical, and for good reason.

Though without proof, Peso suspected Ceaser of snitchin' on Chop. Peso's suspicions that Ceaser was the snitch was aroused by a casual remark Ceaser made the very day of the Green Bay bust which took place over a month ago. Ceaser still owed Chop some money for a drug deal and had not paid him back. As security, Chop had taken Ceaser's Porsche Macan and told him he would only return it when Ceaser paid up. The day of the bust, before Chop's dead body had even reached a morgue and before news of the bust had gotten out, Ceaser went to Chop's house to take back the Porsche. Chop's wife overheard Ceaser say, "He's not gon' be needin' it anymore," and reported it to Peso when he had called her about Chop's death.

"Peso, I'on trust Salvador or either of his sons," Juan outright admitted. He was standing behind the bar pouring himself a drink. "Ceaser could be bad for business."

"Not to mention he's suspected of rattin' out Chop," Raul input. "How the fuck could Ceaser have known so soon that anything had happened to Chop?"

Peso, who was seated on a bar stool, took a swig from his glass of 1800. "An off-the-cuff remark isn't evidence that Ceaser is the one who snitched. We don't have any paperwork to back up our suspicions," he reasoned. "So I wanna give him the benefit of doubt 'cause maybe me and Ceaser can actually do some good business."

"And what about Ceaser's dad? Salvador still hasn't made any effort to come talk with you himself," Raul pointed out. He was sitting atop the bar counter.

"Ceaser's his own man, so I'm sure he don't need his dad's permission to deal with whoever he wants. And sooner or later Salvador and me will have a talk, whether he wants to or not," Peso replied. He checked the time on his bust-down Rolex. "Ceaser should have been here already."

Juan noticed a white Porsche Macan slide to the curb in front of Lu's. He peeped Ceaser step out of the SUV followed by two of his boys, and he could tell they had poles on their persons, judging by the bulges at their waists. "There's Ceaser now. And looks like he brought company," Juan announced. He grabbed the AR-15 from the shelf beneath the bar and sat it on top of the bar counter.

Pulling his Glock .19 equipped with a stick from his waistline, Raul approached the entrance, then unlocked the door and allowed Ceaser along with his boys to enter the place. After her relocked the door behind them, Raul moved over to the bar. As Peso led Ceaser over to a table, he offered him a drink, which Ceaser declined. While Peso's boys were sitting near the bar, Ceaser's boys were posted near the entrance, all of them ready to shoot shit up if caused for. Peso and Ceaser took seats opposite of one another at a table.

"So, what's the business?" Peso cut to the chase.

Ceaser rested his folded his arms atop the table and said, "I need for you to front me ten pounds of smoke."

"Why come to me of all people?" Peso wanted to know.

"Thing is, I struck a deal with a good homeboy of both ours, Marcus. But I'on have the pounds on hand right now so I figured I'd come to you for it. Soon as I get paid, then you'll get paid."

Peso leaned back in his chair, studying Ceaser while mulling over the ordeal. He considered that making the deal could possibly be the start of them conducting more business moving forward. And just maybe he and Salvador could finally talk and gain a mutual understanding.

"I'll tell you what," Peso began. "I'ma front you the pounds. But I expect to be paid within a week." He gulped down some of his tequila.

"You got a deal," Ceaser agreed.

Once their deal was established, Peso told Ceaser that he would meet with him the next day to hand over the pounds, then Ceaser could deliver them to Marcus himself. It was a chain of debt in a convoluted deal.

***

Nearly three weeks had bypassed since the day Peso made the deal with Ceaser, and Ceaser still had not put forth any effort to make good on his end of the bargain. This did not sit well at all with Peso because against his qualm and the objections of Juan and Raul, he still gave Ceaser the benefit of doubt. And yet Peso had not received any benefits.

Peso had fronted Ceaser the ten pings of exotic once the load of his came in through Donnie. And now Peso expected to be paid in full—or, paid in blood.

The Range Rover pulled into the lot of an auto detailing shop with Raul behind its steering wheel, Juan riding shotgun and Peso in the backseat. Raul parked beside Ceaser's Porsche truck, which was being detailed by customer service. Ceaser stood there with his older brother, Junior, waiting on Peso. With the fifty-shot drum of his Glock .45 protruding from under his V-neck T-shirt Peso stepped out of the Range and his boys followed suit.

"Why haven't you come to pay me for the front, Ceaser? Somewhere in the loop, the weed vanished and I never got paid," Peso confronted.

"Peso, I was never paid either," Ceaser claimed. "That's the reason why you never got your paper. 'Cause I ain't finna pay you for some weed that I never seen a dime for."

"You mean to tell me that Marcus got the pounds from you but never paid you for 'em?"

"That's exactly what I'm tellin' you. So you need to take that up with Marcus," Ceaser told him.

Peso eyed him narrowly through Cartier Buffalo lenses. "I'll do that. And I'ma get to the truth," he stated.

Peso nem returned into the Range. He was not sure what to believe at the moment. One thing for sure, he was going to get paid one way or another.

As Raul pulled the whip out of the lot and into South 27th Street traffic he asked, "Peso, you believe Ceaser's keepin' it real with you?"

"I'on believe Ceaser's real at all," Juan interjected.

"It's ways to find out Ceaser's bein' real or not," Peso replied. He pulled out his iPhone and dialed a number.

"Marcus, it's Peso."

"Peso, whassup?" Marcus responded neutrally.

"Whassup is I never got paid from Ceaser, and he claims it's 'cause you never paid him."

Marcus smacked his lips. "Dawg, Ceaser is lyin' through his teeth. I sent him the paper and you should have been paid by now!" he insisted.

"You better be keepin' it real with me Marc, 'cause one of y'all gotta pay," Peso admonished, then ended the call. He needed to get to the truth and knew exactly how to.

"So, what'd Marcus have to say," Raul wanted to know.

"Said Ceaser's a liar 'cause he already paid up."

Juan shook his head and said, "Marcus could be tryin' to help Ceaser finesse you. What you wanna do, lil bro?" He looked into the backseat at Peso.

"I wanna have Marcus snatched up and brought to me."

It was late in the evening when Marcus was just pulling his Audi A4 to the curb. He parked in front of his four bedroom home, where he lived with his wife and two teenage sons. The neighborhood was quiet and safe, for the most part.

Stepping out of his whip, Marcus strolled up the walkway towards the front door of his home. As he began to slide his key into the keyhole, he heard a slight rustling from the neatly trimmed hedges that lined the front of the house. Before he could react it was too late, he felt the press of a muzzle to his left cheekbone, never expecting for anyone to jump from behind the hedges holding him at gunpoint at his own home. Knowing that if he was to try anything, the barefaced gunman would have reason to blow him down on the spot. In order to spare his life, Marcus was inclined to comply to the gunman's demands, which forced Marcus to throw his hands up in surrender. Deep down inside, he knew that Peso sent the hitter.

"Just do as I tell you, and I might let you live," the gunner, who was actually Perry, told him in a cold tone. "Now, take yo' ass over to that car." He jerked the Draco's muzzle towards the stolen KIA Optima that was parked at the curb on the opposite side of the street.

Marcus willingly waltzed over to the vehicle as Perry trailed him while pointing the Draco at his back. Perry forced the nigga to climb his ass inside of the cramped trunk of the car, then slammed the trunk shut before sliding into the driver side behind the steering wheel. He pulled off on the way to bring the hostage to Peso.

Arriving at an abandoned house, where Peso was awaiting inside, Marcus was directed to get out of the trunk by the gunman, then Perry marched him towards the rundown house that looked haunted. Marcus figured this would be where the hitter had planned to leave him dead.

Once Marcus entered the rickety house, there stood Peso, who was flanked by Juan and Raul.

Without speaking a word, Peso pointed toward the lone chair for Marcus to have a seat and, without protest, he did so. Perry used some rope to bind the hostage to the chair, making sure the knots were tightly tied. Marcus did not know what to expect from Peso in the moment, but he sure hoped that he could help resolve the problem.

"Marcus," Peso began coolly. "I consider you a good homeboy of mine, so I hate that it had to come to this. However, I need my fuckin' cheese. So, where is it?" he demanded in a calm manner.

"I kept it real with you, Peso. I sent the money to Ceaser so he should have been paid you," Marcus responded, sticking to his side of the story with hopes that the kingpin take his word.

Peso squatted and met Marcus's eyes. "Can you prove it?"

"Matter fact, I can. I had sent my two sons with the cash and they told me that they personally turned it over to Ceaser. Neither of my sons had ever seen Ceaser before that and they can point him out for you," Marcus explained vehemently.

"Then let's call 'em and have 'em come here now. And if they can point Ceaser out, then I'll let you live," Peso assured.

Once Marcus called up his sons, they agreed to come to the abandoned house if it meant Peso would free their father. When they arrived, Perry frisked them before escorting them inside at gunpoint. The brothers stood near their captive father, willing to do whatever they could to help Marcus.

"All I want is for you to point out to us who you gave the money to," Peso told the brothers.

"Boys, do as he says," Marcus said pleadingly. Peso instructed Perry to stay back with Marcus, then directed the eighteen and nineteen year-old brothers outside and shoved them into the backseat of the KIA Optima behind its tinted windows. The car was driven by Raul with Juan riding shotgun and Peso took up the backseat with the brothers.

Peso had eyes on Ceaser so he knew exactly where to find him. He had one if his boys tailing Ceaser's Porsche truck ever since leaving the auto detailing shop earlier. After running some tasks, Ceaser had driven to a popular food truck on the south side with his people to grab its famous fish tacos.

"As soon as you see the nigga you paid, point him out to Juan and Raul," Peso said to the brothers as they drove towards Ceaser nem. The two teens spotted Ceaser who was with his brother Junior standing at the food truck being serviced, and the teens pointed Ceaser out to them.

"That's him right there!" one of the brothers shouted.

"He's the one we gave the money to!" the second brother confirmed.

The KIA sped around the block. When it came back there were only two men in it—Raul with an AR-15 and Juan with an Kil-Tec .9mm. The KIA slowed to a stop near the food truck just as Ceaser and Junior stepped into the street, fish tacos in hand. One of the shooters fired a burst through the open window, the second over the hood of the KIA.

Boc-boc-boc-boc-boc!

Rrraaa-rrraaa-rrraaa!

Ceaser was popped up twenty-one times and fell backwards onto the sidewalk. Junior was hit twice, once through the liver, and fell head first into the gutter. A ricocheting bullet grazed the forehead of a teenager standing nearby. Ceaser struggled to get to his feet but then fell back and started to crawl. Raul ran up to him and blew out his brains with the AR-15. The shooters jumped back into the KIA and sped away, followed by Peso in another vehicle.

Carlos, a friend of Salvador's, had been driving down South 27th Street—where the food truck was parked—when the shooting happened. Like everybody else, he heard the rapid gunfire and quickly found out what it was about. He drove to Salvador's house and saw Salvador just pulling his Cadillac CTS V wagon into the driveway. Carlos parked at the curb, then stepped out of his car and approached Salvador.

"It's good to see you, Carlos. What brings you by?" It was obvious from the amiable greeting that Salvador had not heard about the deadly shooting.

"I hate to be the one to break the news to you," Carlos began somberly, "But Ceaser's been shot to death and Junior's in pretty bad shape."

Salvador could not believe what he was hearing. "What? When did this happen?"

"A short while ago. I heard the clatter of machine-gun fire and found out what happened once I pulled up on the scene. Thought that I should let you know immediately."

"Take me to the scene," Salvador insisted.

They loaded into Salvador's Cadillac truck and drove to what was now a murder scene teeming with cops. The scene was blocked off by yellow tape and a crime scene team was busied themselves taking photos, marking numerous scattered shell casings and canvassing the area. When Salvador and Carlos approached the scene and let it be known what they were there for, the lead homicide detective allowed them access so that Salvador could identify his youngest son. Once they came near the white sheet covering the corpse and the detective pulled it back, other than a tightening of the jaw and a narrowing of his eyes, Salvador did not display any emotion as he viewed the shredded body of his son.

Carlos had Salvador's boy since birth. He shook his head and said, "Who in the hell could have done this?"

Salvador coldly stated, "I know who did it." He did not elaborate and his longtime friend did not press him. Salvador knew who was behind the murder was none other than Peso.

***

Ceaser's funeral came quickly. The weekend after his murder, his body lay in an open casket in a little chapel in one of the south side's funeral homes.

Mona visited the funeral parlor with she and Peso's young daughter, Maxine. Mona had heard rumors that it was Peso behind Ceaser's murder, but she did not believe it. Peso had Face Timed her from out of town in Miami to assure her it was not so and to ask her to visit the funeral home.

It took a lot of courage for Mona to go to the chapel. When she and Maxi entered and approached the casket, Maxi tugged at her elbow and said, "Mama, Mama, look at him! What's the matter with him?"

Mona broke into tears when she saw Ceaser's baby mama, Yolanda. "I don't know why anybody would have killed Ceaser and done it so awfully," Mona said, dabbing her eyes. "Who did it? Do you know who did it?"

"We already kind of know who did it," Yolanda replied frigidly.

"It wasn't Lupe," Mona responded, sure of it. "Lupe was out of town. He's still out of town. He called me to tell me how sad he was about Ceaser. He asked me to come visit you. You must believe me."

"There's no use you crying now," Yolanda said. "Whoever did it, his turn will come someday. He left my kids without a daddy, and I hope the one who killed Ceaser has kids too, because that is going to leave them without a daddy too, just like he left my children."

Peso's and Ceaser's children had always went to the same daycare and played together and it had always been the joke among the mothers that Peso's daughter Maxine one day would marry CJ, Ceaser's son.

Head bowed, Mona left the funeral home. The women, at any rate, could never be friends again.

CHAPTER 14

With the investigation into the shooting of Ceaser and Junior, Raul was identified as one of the killers. But no one was ever arrested or charged with anything due to lack thereof hardcore evidence.

Peso sent messages to Salvador that they needed to talk following the murder of Ceaser. The messages did not placate Salvador. Salvador was disconsolate over the death of his son and brooded for long periods. It did not take long for word to spread that Ceaser was dead and Junior seriously injured, or for speculation to surface that war had erupted between Peso and Salvador's crews. Everyone expected a showdown. People closed ranks behind Peso or Salvador.

Given Salvador's reputation for ruthlessness, quite a few people figured that Salvador would finish Peso off in short order. But Peso begged to differ.

It was about three in the afternoon on a windy, overcast day when Peso and Raul emerged from Lu's. Having business to tend to, the two were finna head to the stash house, where Juan and other clique members were awaiting. They had driven to the establishment in Peso's BMW truck. As they walked towards the curb, Peso and Raul peeped a navy blue Chevrolet Impala with darkened windows slow down and drive by, as if for a close look at them.

Then, they saw the car back up abruptly and stop in the middle of the street beside Lu's.

"We better get the fuck outta here," Peso urged. He jumped behind the steering wheel clutching his ever-present Glock .45 equipped with a fifty-shot drum and converter switch in hand.

Raul hurried into the passenger side and out the back window, he saw a man with a Tech-9 rush out the Impala, crouch down and take aim. "He's finna bust," Raul yelled as he readied his AR-15. "Swerve off, Peso!"

"Shit!" Peso cursed as he stabbed on the accelerator. The truck sped off just as the gunman opened up.

Prrraaat-prrraaat-prrraaat!

Bullets tore through the BMW's back window, causing Peso and Raul to duck their heads low. An minivan with a man, a woman, and a small girl was coming up National Street. Peso smashed into the side of the vehicle, causing Peso's truck to spin around to the opposite side of the street, throwing him out onto the pavement. Because of all of the blood streaming from Peso's face, Raul feared he was dead.

Raul was not hurt. He slid out of the Beamer truck and crawled up to Peso. The minivan was between them and the shooters, and Raul could see under the BMW that one of the shooters was evidently intending to run across the main street and finish them off at close range. Raul leaned against the truck and visualized where the man would be, then popped up and let off several bursts over the hood of the Beamer.

Rrraa-rrraaa-rrraaa-rrraaa-rrraaa!

As bullets ripped into the gunman's chest, he spun around and then fell on his back. By then, two other assailants were bustin' automatic rifles from across the street.

Raul dragged Peso so that he was protected by the front wheel from bullets that could come from under the BMW. He crouched over Peso's body and busted over the SUV's hood.

One of the ambushers had ducked beside a Volkswagen parked in front of Lu's. With a well-placed burst, Raul cut him down, then ducked back behind the Beamer just as bullets fired by a third shooter slammed violently against the opposite of the truck. Raul looked to his left and saw the man, woman, and little girl who had been in the minivan Peso had collided with. They were hugging the ground and the man was covering the girl with his body. Raul looked to the right and his heart froze when he saw a school bus coming up the street. It was a bus from South Division Highschool, and one of its stops was in front of Lu's.

The bus driver slowed when he saw the wrecked vehicles, then slammed on the brakes when he realized he had driven into the middle of a shootout. Raul could hear the driver screaming at the students to hit the floor. "Get your heads down!" Raul had yelled when several students peered with curiosity out of the window from the back of the bus.

The remaining gunman took advantage of the shield provided by the school bus to drag his wounded comrade into their Impala and jumped behind the steering wheel. He slammed the car into gear and sped down the street with a screech of tires, but Raul was ready for them. The moment the bus came to a stop, Raul had sprinted a few yards to the bus and dropped to the ground behind one of the huge tires. As soon as the fleeing Impala began to speed away, Raul ran out and opened fire with his AR-15.

Rrraa-rrraaa-rrraaa!

The bullets hit their mark. The car zigzagged down the street and crashed into a light pole.

Raul ran back to where Peso was sprawled out and felt for a pulse. He flagged down a passing sedan driven by one of the teachers from the high school. The teacher, a pudgy middle-aged man with dark circles around his eyes, had been on his way home, not far behind the school bus. He was feeling sleepy and longed for a nap. Thinking the bus was stalled from a collision, the teacher stopped to offer to push it to the side of the street. Then, he heard Raul calling him over.

Raul was crouched over Peso's body, nervously looking around for other shooters. In a tone that was more of an order than request, Raul said, "Mister, help me get my homeboy to a doctor."

Like majority of people on the south side, the school teacher knew the name Peso, but he did not know what Peso looked like and did not ask the identity of the injured man. The teacher lifted the kingpin's legs while Raul lifted Peso from underneath the shoulders. Peso was bleeding badly from the scalp and eyebrow. They put Peso into the backseat of the sedan.

The teacher began to realize that he had gotten himself involved in more than a traffic accident when he witnessed Raul retrieve several automatic rifle clips from Peso's wrecked BMW truck and pick up the kingpin's .45 from the street. As he got back behind the steering wheel, the teacher for the first time noticed the body on the other side of the street with round blotches of red on the chest.

"Step on it," Raul ordered after getting into the passenger side. "There may be more of 'em around here."

"What happened?" the teacher ventured as he sped off.

"A bunch of pendejos tried to kill us."

The teacher suddenly felt a chill up and down his spine. He raced throughout traffic, driving through intersections with his horn blaring, eager to get these people where they needed to go as quickly as possible. Raul was looking to the right and to the left and out the back window, as if expecting more carloads of shooters to drive out at any second.

Raul pointed out directions. While they zoomed through traffic, Raul received a call from someone at Lu's who wanted to know if he and Peso was alright. After talking a moment and gathering some information, Raul ended the call. Shortly thereafter, they pulled into the driveway of a brick house with a high wrought-iron fence. The two men lifted Peso from the backseat of the sedan. Peso seemed to be coming around. Mona let out a cry as she opened the front door, and they half-carried Peso into a back bedroom and laid him on a bed. Mona rushed to get a towel and wiped the blood from Peso's face.

"What happened to him?" Mona cried out as she wiped Peso's face with the towel.

"We were caught in an ambush as we came out of Lu's. Some niggas tried to smoke me and Peso," Raul told her.

The teacher realized who the wounded man was when he heard Raul tell the lady what happened to "Peso." For years he had scolded some of his students for imitating the Trap Gods in their dress and speech, but the upbraiding had little to no effect. Now he was in the home of the kingpin of them all. The teacher eyes went from Raul to Peso to the imported French furniture, then to Mona. He realized he had no business there any longer.

"T'm off," the teacher said, heading for the front door.

"Good lookin', Mister," Raul called behind him.

The kindly schoolteacher knew whenever he made it home to his family, then he would be too agitated for the longed-for nap.

Peso soon regained consciousness. As he lifted himself up on his elbows, groggily he said, "Is it over?"

"Yeah Peso, it's over. For now at least. I was able to shoot our way out of the ambush," Raul told him.

"Ah, shit." Peso winced in pain when Mona wiped his face with a towel. Most of the blood was coming from above his eyebrow, where his head had slammed against the steering wheel when in the crash, but a bullet had also creased the top of his skull, and Mona feared his skull was fractured. His head ached terribly. He needed medical attention.

Mona was angry. "Raul, it's your fault this shit happened. I'm certain this was the result of the murder of Ceaser, and now you've gotten Lupe into another shootout. Get the hell out of my house!" she yelled at Raul. But Peso would not hear of it.

"No, he can stay. If it wasn't for him, I'd be dead right now. So, you should be thankin' Raul that I'm even alive, Mona," Peso said bitterly.

Mona stormed out of the room, leaving the man alone. She went to tend to she and Peso's daughter.

"Peso, we need to get you to a hospital and fast," Raul said.

"It won't be a good idea for me to go to any hospital in town," Peso decided. "I'm sure the ambush coulda only been the work of Salvador, and he could have shooters waitin' for me to be taken to one of the hospitals." He had the protection of the DTF to run his drug ring but was on his own when it came to fending off opps.

"Then, I'll drive you to a hospital in Racine," Raul suggested.

"First, I wanna get back at Salvador."

"Peso, we don't even know for sure if he sent those shooters."

"Then, we need to find out, and fast."

"On the drive here, I got a call from Lu's. I was told that a couple of the shooters were hauled off to the hospital."

"We'll go find where the muthafuckas were taken and make 'em talk," Peso said adamantly.

"But first we gotta get you checked out," Raul insisted.

They headed outside and got into Mona's Lexus LX 470 SUV. From there they drove to the small town of Racine, taking the back streets. It was a longer route, but it would be safer than the main streets where ambushers could have been posted.

During the ride, Peso called Juan to let him know what went down. It took about a third of an hour through the back streets to reach the small town. They went to a discreet private clinic where Peso's skull was x-rayed. No fractures were found. The doctor cleaned and sutured the scalp wound and the gash above Peso's eye.

When they stepped out of the clinic, Peso's gangsta side emerged. He wanted the two men in the fleeing Impala that had been taken to the hospital, badly shot up but alive. He got word that one of them died shortly thereafter. The other had been popped eight times, but none of his wounds appeared mortal.

His teeth clinched. Peso said," Let's go back. I wanna get that chocha." He pounded the dashboard emphasizing his frustration.

"Maybe that's not the best idea right now. There's still the chance of another ambush. Let's go to México," Raul suggested as he steered the vehicle.

"Naw, fuck that. I wanna go get that chocha ASAP. I suspect that Salvador's behind the hit, but I wanna find out for sure from the survivin' shooter." Peso was adamant.

At almost eleven o'clock that same night, they made it to Peso's stash spot in Oak Creek. Once they entered the place, Peso quickly roused his brother from bed and rounded up several others, including Perry.

"You good, lil bro?" Juan asked out of concern.

"Yeah, I'm good. But I'll be even better when we take care of this shit," Peso told him. "Let's go and get this nigga."

"Peso, how do you plan to snatch up this nigga? I'm sure he's under police guard in the hospital," Raul pointed out.

"Don't trip, I got a plan," he replied. "Let's bounce."

Peso and his miniature army of dope boys drove in a frenzied rush through the back streets to Milwaukee. Once in town, Peso nem made a stop at Sierra's apartment complex. He stepped out of the Lex' truck and entered the building. When Peso reached Sierra's place, he rapped on the door. A moment later, she answered while barefoot wearing a robe and her hair covered with a silk wrap.

"Peso, what happened to you?" Sierra cared to know, seeing him wrapped in bandages like a mummy.

"Niggas tried to smoke my ass," Peso told her.

"But why?"

"I'll explain that to you later. Right now, I need for you to ride with me. One of the niggas is wounded and in the hospital, and I need you to pose as his sister. All you gotta do is tell them you just got into town and ask for your brother. See how many people they got watchin' the nigga," he asked of her.

Sierra folded her arms beneath her breast and leaned against the doorframe. "Alright, I'll do it for you. But you gotta explain everything to me later," she bargained.

"I will."

Soon thereafter, the miniature army parked near Froederdt hospital. Sierra walked through the Emergency Room entrance. She came out some minutes later. When Sierra returned to the Lex' truck, she reported to Peso that the receptionist told her the guy with gunshot wounds could not have visitors at the moment, and she did see two uniformed police officers outside of his hospital room. Peso was eager to get even so he entered the hospital with Raul, Juan, Perry, and several more of Peso's boys, all of them armed with deadly weapons, poured into the ER corridor.

"We want the dude you have here with the gunshot wounds," Peso demanded. "Where is he?"

One of the nurses pointed upstairs. "Please, don't hurt us."

Peso waved his .45 and said, "You walk in front. Walk!"

When they got upstairs to the room, Peso pushed the nurse in front of him and shouted for the policemen to drop their weapons. At the sight of all the artillery, the policemen had carefully pulled their service weapons out of their holsters and placed them on the floor. Perry collected the weapons. The wounded man, who was hooked up to an oxygen mask and a variety of wires and tubes, woke up. His eyes filled with terror when he saw Peso and his boys standing there with menacing mugs.

A nurse protested, "If you unhook that man, he'll die."

"He's gonna die any fuckin' way," Juan remarked as he carelessly yanked the man's wires and tubes loose.

Peso's boys grabbed the wounded man under the arms and dragged him screaming from the building. They punched him to quiet him down and shoved him into the backseat of the Lex' truck. On the way out to the Oak Creek, they stopped along the highway and Perry tossed the two confiscated service weapons into a sewer. They headed back to the stash house. Raul was driving, Sierra rode in the passenger side and the wounded man was sitting between Peso and Perry in the backseat. He was a young Mexican man with a dark complexion and a thick black mustache. Only the darkness masked his terror. On the way, he told Peso what he wanted to know.

"I wanna know who hired you for the hit on me," said Peso, keeping his tone calm. He spoke in Spanish because the wounded man didn't understand much English.

"It was Salvador," the wounded man admitted in his thick Hispanic accent. "He hired us all the way from México."

"And how much did he pay you to kill me?"

"250,000 pesos each. We needed the money to take care of our families so we took the offer."

"You are a pendejo," Peso snarled. "If you had asked me for that money, I would have given it to you. Now you ain't gon' get to spend that money and neither is your family."

The wounded man was groaning from the pain of his wounds and pleaded for mercy. "Please, spare me. I have children."

"You think I'on have children?" Peso roared, feeling the pain in his skull. "You should have thought about that before. Now it's too late."

Peso's nem SUV rode over plenty of potholes. Juan followed in their tracks in a sedan, then came a third vehicle full of shooters. Peso directed Raul to make a stop at the next gas station. Once they stopped, Peso stepped out of the Lex' and approached the sedan and Juan dashed down his window.

"Whassup?" Juan asked.

"I gotta go and drop Sierra off real quick. So I want you to take the hostage to the stash house," Peso ordered him. "I'll be there right after."

"Don't worry, I'll take care of it."

"Fa sho." Peso returned to the Lex'. "Perry, put this bitch ass nigga in Juan's car so he can take him."

As directed, Perry put the doomed man into the trunk of Juan's sedan. Then, Perry climbed into the passenger seat of the sedan and went along with Juan. They set off to the stash house while Peso had Raul take him to drop Sierra off back at her place. Along the way, he explained everything to her that he was comfortable with her knowing.

"Sierra, good lookin' on what you did for me tonight," Peso said.

"Don't mention it," Sierra replied. "I just don't understand what the hell's going on."

"Some opp of mine sent the shooters at me earlier today with intentions to get rid of me so he can take over the south side. Plus, he believes I had somethin' to do with one of his sons bein' smoked."

Sierra eyed him narrowly. "Do you?" His silence was all the answer she needed. "Peso, you have to stay safe in these streets, or you may not be so lucky next time."

"Right now, for me, stayin' safe means stayin' dangerous," he responded.

"Whatever it takes for you to stay alive."

"Fa sho." Peso shifted in his seat towards her. "I 'preciate you for givin' a fuck about a nigga as much as you do."

"Always." Sierra reached out and gently caressed his wounded head. "Make sure you take care of this before it gets worse."

"It looks a lot worse than it is. But I'll be sure to take care of it."

Once they pulled up in front of Sierra's apartment complex, she leaned over and pecked Peso on his lips. Before exiting the vehicle, she made Peso promise to call her later on. After dropping Sierra off, Peso and Raul drove on to the stash house with their shooters tailing.

Soon thereafter, they arrived at the stash house and Peso was eager to continue with his interrogation on the wounded man. He and Raul stepped out of the Lex' truck and headed for the front door. "Where's the hostage?" Peso asked Juan once he stepped into the front room. He still had some questions for the wounded man.

"We murked his bitch ass. His end wasn't very pleasant either. We already tossed his body in a dumpster for the maggots to finish off," Juan informed.

Peso was pissed off. "I wanted to question him more, and I wanted to kill him my fuckin' self!" he yelled.

"Hermano," Juan said apologetically. "I thought you had already asked him everything you needed to ask him earlier."

"Don't even trip on it." Peso took a seat on the couch beside his brother. "At least I did get him to tell me that the one who hired 'em to smoke me is Salvador."

Raul asked, "Now what do you wanna do about it?"

"When the timing is right," Peso began in a stoic manner, "Then, I'll deal with Salvador."

CHAPTER 15

Subsequent to the shooting in front of Lu's, Peso began taking more precautions. While at Lu's, he surrounded himself with more shooters than ever before and most times he traveled around with carloads of shooters. The shootout in front of Lu's was just the first round.

Peso had always been eager to exchange drugs for weapons and ammunition, but now acquiring a huge arsenal had become a necessity in order to arm all of the new recruits. Both sides seemed to be recruiting for a showdown. One of Peso's younger cousins, Chato, abandoned life in México to enlist in Peso's cause. A morose, chipped-tooth man, Chato told his relatives in México that he was going to the United States and did not know if he would ever see them again, but he was going to join his cousin.

Being that there was a war between Peso and Salvador, Milwaukee's south side was bound to rage with violence.

Behind the stash house, Peso, along with Raul, Juan, Perry and Chato, stood there as a sedan pulled up driven by Donnie. Donnie had come to drop the latest load off to Peso. He had been smuggling at least two loads a week out of México. His job consisted of driving the product to its destination, sometimes collecting the money, and bringing either the product or money back to Peso. It was so much easier making money this way, though Donnie had to recognize that all the violence and killing was beginning to scare him, even more than the thought of gettin' arrested.

Stepping out of the sedan, Donnie approached Peso, who was flanked by his boys, and said, "The load's stashed beneath the floorboards."

"Chato, how 'bout you and Perry take the load out," Peso instructed and the two began unloading the cargo from the sedan's stash spot. He returned his focus on Donnie. "Good lookin' on deliverin' this load. Shit has been so crazy lately with the beef between me and Salvador that I haven't been able to move much work."

"Peso, I ain't gon' lie, the beef between y'all scares the hell outta me. I've known Ceaser nem for a while. I even kicked it with 'em before. And you my homeboy, I respect you. But I ain't tryin' to get caught up in the middle of an unending bloodbath," Donnie expressed circumspectly.

"I can understand that Donnie. I'on expect for you to pick a side; I just expect you to understand that my side rules," Peso told him.

After the product was unloaded from the sedan, Donnie returned behind its steering wheel and pulled off. Peso really did understand where Donnie was coming from in regard to his beef with Salvador, which placed Donnie between a rock and a hard place. Although, Peso would smoke whoever sided with Salvador.

Once the product was taken into the stash house, Peso and the others prepared packages for where they had to go. There were a few trap spots and a couple of trappers that were in need of some work.

"Juan, take this work to Greedy and the other spots," Peso asked of his brother. He had another block of boy going to Greedy, and more boy and weed going elsewhere.

"I got'chu, lil bro," Juan said. He stood from his seat at the table and grabbed the Dior backpack, which contained the product.

"You make sure to be on point in those streets with Salvador's steppers out there lurkin'," Peso forewarned.

Juan grabbed the Draco off the table. "That's why I keep the Drac' with me. Plus, I'ma have Perry nem with me just in case."

"Just return here after you drop the work off. Me, Raul and Chato gon' be here still preppin' the sacks."

"Then, I'll see you when I make it back," Juan assured. Then he, Perry, and three more shooters made their way out of the stash house. The small gang piled into Juan's Infiniti truck, all of them toting blicks.

Cartel Money

The first stop Juan nem would make was to meet up with Greedy. There were a pack of niggas flanking Greedy when Juan nem pulled into the parking lot of Wing Stop. By now, Greedy had gotten his money up so he felt the need to surround himself with more shooters. Juan parked his Infiniti truck beside Greedy's newly purchased blue passion mica colored Maserati Quattroporte S Q4 Granlusso. With a bag containing the brick of boy in hand, Juan stepped out of his whip, and Perry followed suit with his Draco in hand. As Juan and Greedy conducted business, Perry closely observed Greedy's gang, mainly Spider.

"Here's the brick of dawg food. Just make sure you run Peso his paper ASAP for the front," Juan advised.

Greedy leaned back up against his new whip and stated, "I'ma pay Peso whenever I get the cheese to. Ain't like I'ma run off on the plug."

"If you even think about doin' some shit like that, then we gon' shoot up that nice ass car of yours until we flip it."

"Take it easy, Juan. I'm just talkin' shit." Greedy made clear.

"Well, I ain't. Like I said, have that money for Peso soon." Without warning, Juan turned and jumped back into the Infiniti truck and Perry followed.

After dropping the product off to Greedy and the other spots, Juan nem were riding up Greenfield

Street on the way back to the stash spot. They were talkin' shit among each other while passing around a blunt of gas as EST Gee's track "Pray You Die In Surgery" played in the background.

During the ride, Juan peeped some opps, and told his boys, "There goes some of Salvador's crew. Y'all niggas be ready to bust."

Two of Salvador's men were parked in a Chevrolet Equinox in front of a liquor store. A junkie was in the backseat being served some dope by one of the men. As they were finna get out, the Infiniti truck suddenly raced up and Juan nem opened fire with Dracos, AR-15s and Glocks.

Boc-boc-boc-boc-boc!

Rrraa-rrraaa-rrraaa!

Blam-blam-blam-blam-blam!

The three shooters, who rode along with Juan and Perry, had jumped out of the Infiniti and the guns jerked in their hands from the recoil as they fanned down the Equinox. Juan and Perry were bustin' from behind opened doors of the Infiniti. The combined gunfire created a tremendous roar and sent a thick cloud of gun smoke billowing into the night sky.

All that saved Salvador's two men was the arrival of another one of his men, who emerged from the liquor store strapped with a Glock .27 equipped with a fifty-shot drum. He busted at Juan nem while they were fannin' down the Equinox. Two of Juan's shooters fell before they even realized they were being bushwhacked. Urgently, the others scrambled into the Infiniti and sped away, taking a few last shots at the Equinox before their vehicle skidded around a corner.

Along with two dead bodies, an AR-15 and more than two-hundred shells was in the street and a count of seventy-eight bullet holes in Salvador's men Equinox. The two men had been popped up half a dozen times each and were in serious condition. The junkie, who had ducked to the floorboards when the shooting started, miraculously survived without a scratch.

Following the shooting, Juan Face Timed Peso to let him know what was up. But Peso did not take the news like they expected he would. He was upset about the shooting, particularly with Juan.

"Hell do you mean that y'all slid on some of Salvador's boys," Peso said frustrated. "Told you that I'll deal with Salvador."

"But, Peso, if you keep puttin' it off, then he'll try to have you smoked again!"

Peso scolded Juan by replying, "The beef is between me and Salvador. Why should anyone else pay for somethin' that is between me and another man?"

"It shouldn't matter who the fuck it is! If they're with him, then they're against you!"

"Hermano, I understand your point of view. Trust me, I'll deal with Salvador. For now, let's just focus on chasin' a bag."

After ending the call with Peso, Juan needed to go and clear his head. *I'on understand why Peso's holdin' back from slidin' on Salvador*, he contemplated. If it was up to me, I would send a gang of shooters at Salvador daily 'til he's dead. But Juan would respect his brother's mind and do things Peso's way instead.

Rather than return directly to the stash house with Peso and the others, Juan and Perry detoured to a strip joint. They had some drinks and received lap dances all night. At three in the morning when almost everybody except the diehard revelers like Juan had gone home, Juan and Perry came stumbling out of the club. When they reached the parking lot, blinding head lights shined on them and suddenly shots erupted.

Rrraa-rrraaa-rrraaa-rrrraaa!

When the vehicle sped out of the parking lot, Juan was left crawling to the entrance of the club on all fours with blood streaming from his chest. He died before reaching the door. His young shooter Perry was killed as he ran to Juan's Infiniti truck for his Draco. The others fled away and left them for dead.

Salvador's shooters later boasted while live on the 'Gram that they were behind those slayings. They imitated shooting their guns at the camera and threatened that Peso would be next.

After Juan was killed, Peso's boys retaliated and two days later, three dead bodies were found in an alley. Each had been shot twice in back of the head. One of the dead men was one who bragged about smokin' Juan online, a cousin of Salvador's.

What started with the murder of Ceaser transformed the south side into a murder zone.

CHAPTER 16

It was a magnificent view from the balcony of the Hilton hotel suite, which overlooked Cancun. Peso, along with Sierra, had flown first-class out to México in order to get away for a few nights. It had been Sierra who insisted they take the trip, convincing Peso that he needed some time away from the streets.

Damn, I'm gainin' status in the streets but losin' a lot of people close to me, Peso mused crestfallen. While Peso stood out on the balcony as the sun beamed down, he could not help but to contemplate on all of the losses he had suffered thus far. He lost his father Luis, brother Juan, and his homeboy Suave, plus others along the way. And now during the war with Salvador, Peso was sure there would be even more losses to come. All due to money, power and respect. By any means, he thought introspectively, the war between me and Salvador has to come to an end.

Appearing in the doorway of the balcony, Sierra stood there wearing a plush Terry cloth robe. She could read that Peso was lost in thought, and she wanted to change his mind. Sierra stepped out onto the balcony and stood right beside him. She also drank in the magnificent view.

"I didn't convince you to come all the way here just so you could think about the streets back home," Sierra mentioned.

"My guess is you convinced me to come here so that you can have me all alone," Peso replied, fondling her with his eyes.

"Actually, I convinced you to come here so that you can relax. But... I don't mind having some time alone with you."

"Then, why don't you do somethin' to help me relax?"

Peso wrapped his arms around her small waist and pulled her into his chest. He kissed her neck and she rested her head against his chest and pressed her perky breasts against him. He licked her earlobe and gently caressed her phat ass.

"Mmmmm, Peso," Sierra moaned as he peeled the robe off of her body, exposing her brown skin. Once the robe fell onto the floor at their feet, she stood there in only lingerie.

Sierra began to grind against him. Peso matched her movements. His dick was brick from excitement inside of his Nike jogger pants. Peso slid down her boy shorts. Sierra kicked her undergarment onto one side of the balcony. He turned her around, bent her over, and she placed both hands on the rail. Licking his full lips, he knelt behind her. Sierra's pussy was right in his face. It was cleanly shaven with pinkish flesh. Using both his thumbs, Peso spread her pussy lip apart, then slid his warm tongue over her clitoris.

Sierra gasped as his tongue pleased her love box. She threw her head back. The stimulation was better than ever before. Peso continued to slip his thick tongue in and out of her wet pussy as he also massaged her slit with two fingers.

Sierra moaned loudly and gripped the railing. "Oooh, that shit feels so fuckin' amazing, boy. Yaaas, Peso!" He buried his face in her ass and put his whole mouth over her pussy from behind and gave it a passionate tongue-kiss. As he flicked his tongue over her clit, he spread her lips wider and finger-fucked her. Her legs grew weak and her frame began to quiver as she groaned and panted aloud. Her entire body trembled as her cum gushed all over his handsome face. "Yaaaas!" Sierra said breathlessly as she collapsed against the railing.

Peso stood and took off his jogger pants, and then he sat down in the large white balcony chair. Sierra peered back at him over her shoulder. She watched him stroke his big, hard dick as he viewed her toned brown thighs, her phat ass, and her puckered pussy lips. "Come and get all this dick," he enticed. Once she stepped close, he pulled her to him by her small waist and kissed her flat tummy. "Damn lil baby, a nigga wanna feel you so bad. How 'bout you sit on this dick and ride it."

Sierra did not hesitate to mount his lap. She gently bit her lower lip as she eased down on his thick piece. Her wetness invited him inside of her with ease. Peso gripped her ass as he felt her slit tighten around his meat. She paused, locked eyes with him and offered him a seductive smirk. She pushed him back, leaned forward, and planted her hands on his chest. Peso sucked her erect nipples and, without saying a word, Sierra began pouncing her wet shot on his dick.

"Yeah, boo! Damn!" Peso grunted as her sexy pussy adored his dick, making it sensitive with each bounce of her soft ass. A nut swelled up in the tip of his sensitized dick and he released his sperm.

Both of them laid back on the large balcony chair panting. It was not long before room service came knocking at their suite door. Sierra climbed off of Peso's lap, grabbed up her robe and slipped it on, covering her nakedness. She left Peso to gather himself while she went to collect the dinner they ordered some time before their raunchy sex scene. She wheeled the cart out onto the balcony, where they would eat.

While the couple enjoyed their meals, the burning sun was beginning to sink into the horizon, causing a streak of orange and crimson to form across the sky.

"México is a very beautiful place," Sierra complimented as she took in the view and forked a piece of tender baby goat meat.

"Believe me, you haven't even seen the most beautiful parts of this country," Peso promised her. "This is the land my dad was from, where he grew up. He brought me here many times, and each time he told me pieces of its history."

"I'm sure your dad was proud to be from here."

"Tomorrow, I'll show you the little village he grew up in. It's a very humblin' place, but it made him who he was." Peso took a drink from his glass of tequila.

***

The following day Peso had arranged for he and Sierra to be taken to where his father Luis had been born and raised, the village of Santa Elena. They took a small aircraft, which flew them over some of the deserts and mountains of México. Soon, they were descending and landed on a dirt road near the village.

The village was situated on a stony chunk of desert, and it was near the Rio Grande. Directly behind the village and stretching for miles to the east and west were the 1,800-foot cliffs of Sierra Ponce, a limestone mass that had surged from the ground in some tectonic cataclysm eons ago. Five miles upstream, the Rio Grande flowed out of a canyon and meandered into the river valley. The river village had farms with cows and goats and gardens with corn and beans. Many of the villagers lived in adobe shacks.

As they strolled through the village, Peso was greeted in Spanish by the villagers that had known him since his father used to bring him there as a child. He led Sierra to the burial grounds of his father, which was a small graveyard. Being that Luis was from the village, his widowed wife and children decided to have him buried there.

"The saga of my dad, Luis Martinez, is the story of thousands of Mexicana borderland people who learned to survive by their wits in the midst of a harsh desert environment," Peso began. He and Sierra stood before Luis's tombstone. "When the desert farms failed to produce enough food, migrant farm work in the United Sates or petty smuggling, sometimes both, allowed many familias to survive.

"My dad decided to move to the states for a better chance at life. That's when he eventually met my mama. They had three children, includin' me, and were happily married. I'll be the first to admit that my dad wasn't at all perfect, but neither was he a bad person. My dad just did what was necessary to take care of la familia," he expressed. "And I'm only doin' the same."

Sierra interlocked her petite fingers with his, and gingerly said, "Peso, your dad sounds like he was a good person. Nobody's perfect."

"You right," he agreed. "Sometimes I wonder what life would be like had my dad brought us here to live instead."

"Have you ever considered leaving Milwaukee and moving here?"

"Maybe someday. But I still have a life there that I can't just leave behind."

"Well, I just fear that your life will be cut short with the way you're living," Sierra uttered.

Peso met her sincere eyes and admitted, "I'on live my life with that sort of fear."

The two spent some time around the village with some of its natives and listened to stories about Luis as a child from some of the elders. Afterwards, they were flown back to Cancun and returned to their hotel. Peso felt comfortable in the company of Sierra. He enjoyed having her within his presence. And Sierra thoroughly appreciated that he felt comfortable enough to have her around. She was getting to know some about him although, realistically, she did not know the half about Peso.

***

While Peso left Sierra at the hotel to enjoy a day at the spa, he had went to Mexico City to meet with his connect, Tito. Peso figured that while he was already visiting the country he might as well cease the opportunity to rendezvous with the kingpin of the Mexican Cartel.

Tito had invited Peso to his fortress of a home. The mansion sat on twenty-two acres of land and was surrounded by a large golden gate. There were all kinds of statues and bushes trimmed into different shapes of animals around the landscape. The two men sat at a patio table outside near the huge underground swimming pool. A maid served them some stiff drinks. Old man Tito was only wearing silk pajamas and slippers designed by Gucci and a very expensive Patek timepiece on his arm. For an elderly gentleman, he was very fit and incredibly sharp. Stories describe him to be ruthless. However, Tito was down to earth.

"I'm told that you've been doing quite well with business in America," Tito said, speaking in Spanish.

"Besides a few issues, business is good," Peso replied in Spanish.

"Excellent. Maybe I should grant you more product. I trust that you will not disrespect me like that son of a bitch Cobra." The kingpin shook his head in disgust. He still wanted to dead Cobra behind the loss of his money and his nephew.

Peso shifted towards him in his seat. "Señor Tito, Cobra killed a good friend of mine so I understand your anger towards him. And trust me, my respect for you will never allow me to do you wrong."

"Lupe, I've been doing this a very long time now. And of the many men I've met over the years, you are the epitome of the Mexican Cartel."

"I'm humbled that you feel such a way, Señor Tito."

"With that said, I will be sure to entrust you with more product for your operation." Tito took a swig from his glass of 1800. "Now, how about we enjoy our drinks and talk about life."

The assignation with the kingpin himself had secured Peso more product and prestige. He realized that he would have to guard his position, because there will be others out to take his position for themselves.

CHAPTER 17

"We can't do shit, Peso! He's a thorn in the side. You need to either talk to him or kill him."

Chato, Peso's younger cousin, listed the options just after Peso returned from his trip to México, echoing the opinion of everybody else in their crew. The murders were making everybody uneasy. Salvador seemed hellbent on vengeance until either Peso was dead or Salvador himself was killed. And a lot of people could die—were already dying—in the process.

They were gathered at Lu's holding the discussion pertaining to Salvador. Along with Peso and Chato, Raul and others were present. Peso looked around in the faces of his boys, he could read that they wanted Salvador dead. But he favored a deal. As far as he was concerned, it was time to bury the dead and move on. He was motivated by pragmatism: the shootouts were causing pressure to be applied by local authorities. Shootouts in broad daylight was costing Peso money because product could not be moved.

By the time he came back from his trip to México, Peso had decided it was time for a showdown. Either he and Salvador work out their differences once and for all, or they shoot it out and see who lives to tell the story later.

"Today will be the day I deal with Salvador," Peso told his boys.

"I'll kill him myself if it comes to that," stated Chato.

Peso objected. "Naw, lil cuz. Let's go over and talk and see what happens."

Peso carefully selected men to go with him, his younger cousin, Chato, his protégé, Felix, Paulie, the half-brother of Juan's shooter Perry; and the fifth man was an ambitious shooter named Burns. More carloads of shooters would have been perceived as a provocation, as would the presence of Raul, who was suspected of murdering Salvador's son, Ceaser, so Peso made a point to leave him out of it.

Before heading out to Salvador's house, Peso took his small army to his stash house, where they collected artillery and bulletproof vests. While the others were armed with AR-15s and Dracos, Peso had his Glock .45 equipped with a fifty-shot drum, and its converter switch to made the handgun shoot like a mini assault rifle. Despite the summer heat, they donned the bulletproof vests.

Peso did not want to leave anything to chance. He went himself in order to scout out Salvador's crib, sitting in an inconspicuous white Mazda CX-3 behind tinted windows along with his team on the block down the street from the house. In the driveway sat parked Salvador's Cadillac CTS V wagon. There was a second vehicle parked at the curb in front of the house. Salvador's home was in the center of the block with fence around its lawn. The neighborhood was quiet.

Peso surveyed the streets. In one direction, it was a one-way street that lead to a main street. The other street was a dead end.

A woman emerged from the house with her children and they made their way to the vehicle parked at the curb. Peso recognized her as Yolanda, Ceaser's baby mama. She and her kids entered the vehicle and departed under the gaze of Peso's surveillance. That only left Salvador, his wife Maria and a lady friend of hers at the house, so far as Peso could tell.

Following Yolanda's departure, Peso and his boys abandoned their surveillance post and decided to pull up at the house prepared for a showdown. Felix was not a very good shot, so Peso had him drive. Once they reached the block leading to Salvador's home, Felix guided the Mazda SUV down the street while everyone else kept a tense eye out for an ambush in one of the gangways in between the houses lining the block on either side.

As they approached the house, Peso said to Felix, "Drive around the block first. I wanna make sure no one is hiding anywhere." After driving around the block and seeing nothing suspicious, the white Mazda stopped directly in front of the house at the curb. They tensed when they saw Maria, Salvador's wife, peer out the front door.

"What do you want?" Maria scowled. She, a stout, strong-willed woman who had bore and raised six children, stepped out alone and stood in front of the half-opened door. "What are you going to do, kill me too?"

"I wanna talk to Salvador," Peso requested.

"He's not here. He's out of town."

Peso could see that she was nervous and was convinced Salvador was inside. Salvador's vehicle was in the driveway, surely he was there now. Peso knew it. The kingpin walked towards the house alone, his Glock in hand. His boys were covering him from behind. He knew Salvador would not shoot with Maria standing there. She would be dead just a few seconds after Peso.

Peso pointed to the Cadillac in the driveway. "I know Salvador is here. I've been layin' on you. I saw Yolanda leave not too long ago with two children. I know your husband is here at the house, probably with some of his men. If that muthafucka want gunplay, tell his ass let's do it now and get it over with," he spoke loudly, thinking that Salvador was within earshot. "If you don't wanna beef anymore, tell Salvador let's squash the beef and make money."

"Salvador is not here," Maria said once more. "He hasn't been here all day. God up above knows I'm telling you the truth."

There were a couple of chairs on the porch near the door. Peso shoved his .45 into his waistband and sat down. He motioned to the other chair. "Sit down. We have to talk."

She shook her head and folded her arms defiantly. "No."

"We have to put an end to this shit," he said. "I know that you think I killed Ceaser, but I didn't. And neither did my brotha Juan. Yeah, it was my nigga, but I wasn't there when he did it. But he did it, and I can't take that back."

Maria had heard this before and did not believe it. She felt like Peso was not sincere because he still kept Raul around. All the anger began to spill out in her voice. "You may not have done it with your own gun, but you sent them to do it," she said, her voice quivering. "Compared to you and the one who killed him, he was just a boy. He was just a defenseless boy, and he did not owe you any money."

"You're wrong and there has been a lot of blood because you're wrong," Peso remarked. He noted the determination in Maria's dark eyes.

He enumerated the people who had died on both sides because she was wrong. There was Juan and Juan's shooter, Perry. There were the three men left dead in the alley, one being Salvador's cousin. Two of Salvador's men had been seriously wounded in front of the liquor store. Then there were the men Salvador hired from México to kill Peso who lost their lives. Several of Peso's boys were left slain. There was already much blood on both sides in the balance.

"Why don't we squash the beef before we lose more people," Peso said.

Salvador's wife shook her head.

"Do you think you would sleep better at night if you kill me?"

"Yes, I do," Maria replied sternly.

Emotions flashed within Peso's eyes. When Maria saw the raw emotion, she thought that Peso had for the first time understood the enormity of what he started and that excuses and apologies were of no use. There was no turning back. It was just too damn late.

Peso could feel the sun beating down. Underneath the bulky bulletproof vest was like an oven, and sweat was rolling down his torso. He reached for his waist and in a flash pulled his Glock .45 from his YSL belt. He chambered a round and handed it to her. She took the pole by the handle, but held it limply. "If you think that will bring back Ceaser, then kill me. All you gotta do is..." he said, crooking his trigger finger.

Maria looked at the black semiautomatic. Here was the opportunity she had longed for to avenge her son's death. The slightest pressure on the trigger now would fire the weapon. But when she looked up over Peso's shoulder, she could see his boys in the Mazda at the curb. The SUV was bristling with machine guns. Peso's boys had jerked to attention when he handed Maria his blick, and all of them were staring at her. Quite possibly for a brief moment Peso had forgotten about his boys, but Maria knew she would have only seconds to live herself if she were to take him up on his offer.

Maria handed the pistol back. "This is not how I'm going to kill you, Lupe," she said, trembling with rage.

"But isn't this what you want, is to kill me?" Peso pressed.

"And one day soon it will happen."

The lady friend came out of the house and whispered something to Maria, who went into the house and returned moments later. Her expression had changed. She seemed as inflexible as ever but more willing to talk. Peso suspected that Salvador had gone out the backdoor and that her lady friend told Maria to stall Peso for time.

They continued the futile dialogue a short while longer. Peso grew angry at her intransigence. He swore at her and strode back to the Mazda SUV. As he climbed into the passenger side, he shouted: "If Salvador don't wanna squash the beef, you tell his ass we gon' spin on him when he least expects it."

Peso told Felix to take the side street out. He figured that if Salvador had managed to organize his crew for an ambush while he was talking with Maria, it would along the main street. Though more traffic, it offered a better position for an ambush.

The Mazda pulled away from the curb and down the street. As they approached the corner, they saw a forest green Buick Enclave coming towards them barely hundred yards away.

"We gotta stop that fuckin' truck. Maybe it's Salvador," Peso urged.

The Buick was driven by Salvador's friend, Carlos, who happened to be unknowingly heading into an ambush that Salvador had prepared for Peso. Carlos was on his way to pick up his wife, Maria's lady friend.

While Peso was pleading with Maria to squash the beef, Salvador and a cousin of his had gotten to the end of the block, hoping Peso would leave along the side street. Bent over and carrying machine guns, Salvador and his cousin had scurried through the alley behind the house and took up position on each side of the street.

As the Mazda approached the Buick, Salvador and his cousin jumped out of gangways and opened fire.

Rrraaa-rrraaa-rrraaa!

Boc-boc-boc-boc-boc!

Peso and Felix saw it as if in slow motion. Salvador had scrambled to his feet, stood straight up, naked from the waist up, jammed the rifle stock into his shoulder and squeezing the rifle grip with the other hand. He was cutting loose with a stream of bullets that blew one of the front tires, tore into the

166

radiator, and ripped across the window, spraying glass and bullet fragments everywhere.

Inside the crowded Mazda, five men groaned, screamed, and cursed as the terror of death gripped them. Peso and Felix had instinctively ducked toward the center, banging heads as they scrambled to get under the shelter of the dashboard. Peso's forehead was peppered with broken glass. A bullet had creased his right eyebrow and another his skull, and he could feel warm blood trickling down his face. In the backseat, several bullets slammed into Chato's bulletproof vest and knocked him backwards.

Paulie, meanwhile, dived for the floorboards. He was able to slide his arm up to the handle of his door and shove the door open. He stuck his AR-15 under the door and shot wildly to keep anyone from running up on the Mazda to finish them off.

Prrrat-prrrat-prrrat!

A bullet from the assault rifle struck Salvador's cousin in the shoulder, and impact had thrown him to the ground, knocking the wind out of him. As the cousin climbed to his feet, he saw both Salvador and Carlos bustin' at the Mazda. Throwing his AK-47 onto the ground, he ran for his life.

Carlos had jumped in on the action. When he realized what was happening, he had hurried out of the Buick with a handgun and took aim at Peso's nem's Mazda and begun airin' it out.

Chato had been stunned by the impact of bullets to his vest but quickly recovered his senses.

He swung his Draco over Peso's head and fired with a deafening roar through the windshield, showering Peso with a stream of hot cartridge shells and broken glass.

Blocka-blocka-blocka-blocka!

Chato took aim first at Salvador, then at Carlos standing near the Buick that had stopped on the other side of the street. One of Chato's bullets hit Carlos in the head and he fell to the ground next to the Buick. His blood and brain matter splattered on its paint job. The bullet tore a gaping, triangular chunk from Carlo's cranium.

Salvador had made a fatal mistake. Once he had pulled the trigger, he did not let up until he had expanded the entire fifty-round clip. That's when Peso raised up and stuck his Glock .45 out the front window, then he let off rapid gunfire.

Boom-boom-boom-boom!

"Argh, shit!" They heard Salvador yelp and he dropped onto the pavement.

Suddenly, the block was silent. Peso, his face covered in blood, got out of the Mazda truck cautiously. He had never come so close before to the reality of death. He was both nauseated by his bloody wounds and ferociously elated that he survived. The kingpin and his mob were in a savage frenzy. Peso walked up to Salvador, who was sprawled on the ground, chasing his breath. Peso stood over Salvador with his .45 and looked him in the eyes before he was to die, without no feelings for him. Peso squeezed the trigger.

Boom-boom-boom-boom!

Salvador's body jerked from each shot. He was left breathless.

Felix was trembling. "Peso," he said, "There's another one but I don't know where he went."

"Go look for the other shooter," Peso instructed Chato and Paulie. After searching the immediate area, they reported that they only found an AK-47 lying in the gangway and blood drops showing the man had ran off. Peso told his boys, "I believe Salvador set up another ambush, and they will attempt to intercept us on the main street. For our own protection, we have to get the Salvador's bitch. They won't ambush us if we have her."

Peso at the steering wheel, they commandeered Carlo's Buick and headed back to Salvador's house. For their own protection, Peso realized they needed to go back to the home to take hostages. He also called Raul, ordering more shooters to meet him in front of Salvador's house.

As they approached the house, they spotted Maria and her lady friend, walking toward the Cadillac truck parked in the driveway. When the women saw Carlos's Buick approaching, their faces broke into broad smiles. They did not recognize Peso's bloodied face until he screeched to a halt and jumped out.

Peso was bleeding profusely. He wiped the blood from his eyes and grabbed Maria by the arm. He shook her violently, and said sarcastically,

"Goin' somewhere? Lemme give you a ride." He slapped her ferociously and shoved her and her lady friend into the backseat of Salvador's Cadillac truck with Chato and Paulie. Felix rode shotgun.

Peso would take the Cadillac because the Mazda's tire was flattened and both of the vehicles present during the shooting had leaked all of the coolant through bullet holes in the radiator, and the motors would begin to give out. By now, a carload of Peso's shooters pulled up. Once Peso and the others pulled off, the shooters fell behind the Cadillac truck.

"You thought I was the one that died. I saw that in your face," Peso said with sinister glee. "But I wasn't the one who died. Do you wanna know who was the one who died? I'ma show you." He slowed the truck near the corner. All that was visible of Salvador were his Air Force 1s as his breathless body lay behind a parked car. With a bloodstained finger, Peso pointed to the body. "Salvador wasn't at the house?" he asked rhetorically.

"No," Maria replied sadly.

"Then, who in the hell is that?"

"I don't know."

"You know who the hell it is. You sent him to kill me. And you're responsible for his death. We Swiss-cheesed his ass," Peso said with a low, guttural, unnatural laugh.

Maria put her face in her hands and began to weep. As they headed towards the main street, they passed the body of Carlos, a burly man of forty-two, Maria's lady friend husband, lying face down in the street. It was the lady friend's turn to weep.

They drove toward Peso's stash house in Oak Creek. On the way, he warned, "If somebody tries to shoot me before I reach my destination, I'ma shoot you first. You're gonna die before I do." He was convinced Salvador's shooters were still on the lookout for him and would try to ambush him, but he knew they would not try anything as long as Maria was his hostage. Once they were in the clear, Peso took Maria and her friend into an alleyway. He forced them out of the Cadillac truck and made them kneel.

Boom! Boom!

Peso shot both of the women in back of their heads, execution style.

With Salvador's demise, Peso appeared to be formidable, untouchable, ferocious—a warning to would-be rivals. Now Peso could sit back and revel in his fame as the kingpin of Milwaukee's south side's Cartel.

To Be Continued...

Martell "T" Bolden

172

Lock Down Publications and Ca$h Presents
Assisted Publishing Packages

BASIC PACKAGE	UPGRADED PACKAGE
$499	$800
Editing	Typing
Cover Design	Editing
Formatting	Cover Design
	Formatting
ADVANCE PACKAGE	**LDP SUPREME PACKAGE**
$1,200	$1,500
Typing	Typing
Editing	Editing
Cover Design	Cover Design
Formatting	Formatting
Copyright registration	Copyright registration
Proofreading	Proofreading
Upload book to Amazon	Set up Amazon account
	Upload book to Amazon
	Advertise on LDP, Amazon and Facebook Page

***Other services available upon request.
Additional charges may apply
Lock Down Publications
P.O. Box 944
Stockbridge, GA 30281-9998
Phone: 470 303-9761

Submission Guideline

Submit the first three chapters of your completed manuscript to ldpsubmissions@gmail.com, subject line: Your book's title. The manuscript must be in a .doc file and sent as an attachment. Document should be in Times New Roman, double spaced and in size 12 font. Also, provide your synopsis and full contact information. If sending multiple submissions, they must each be in a separate email.

Have a story but no way to send it electronically? You can still submit to LDP/Ca$h Presents. Send in the first three chapters, written or typed, of your completed manuscript to:

LDP: Submissions Dept
Po Box 944
Stockbridge, Ga 30281

DO NOT send original manuscript. Must be a duplicate.

Provide your synopsis and a cover letter containing your full contact information.

Thanks for considering LDP and Ca$h Presents.

NEW RELEASES

SOSA GANG 2 by ROMELL TUKES
KINGZ OF THE GAME 7 by PLAYA RAY
SKI MASK MONEY 2 by RENTA
BORN IN THE GRAVE 3 by SELF MADE
TAY
LOYALTY IS EVERYTHING 3 by MOLOTTI

Coming Soon from Lock Down Publications/Ca$h Presents

BLOOD OF A BOSS **VI**
SHADOWS OF THE GAME II
TRAP BASTARD II
By Askari
LOYAL TO THE GAME **IV**
By T.J. & Jelissa
TRUE SAVAGE **VIII**
MIDNIGHT CARTEL IV
DOPE BOY MAGIC IV
CITY OF KINGZ III
NIGHTMARE ON SILENT AVE II
THE PLUG OF LIL MEXICO II
CLASSIC CITY II
By Chris Green
BLAST FOR ME **III**
A SAVAGE DOPEBOY III
CUTTHROAT MAFIA III
DUFFLE BAG CARTEL VII
HEARTLESS GOON VI
By Ghost
A HUSTLER'S DECEIT III
KILL ZONE II
BAE BELONGS TO ME III
TIL DEATH II

Cartel Money

By Aryanna
KING OF THE TRAP III
By T.J. Edwards
GORILLAZ IN THE BAY V
3X KRAZY III
STRAIGHT BEAST MODE III
De'Kari
KINGPIN KILLAZ IV
STREET KINGS III
PAID IN BLOOD III
CARTEL KILLAZ IV
DOPE GODS III
Hood Rich
SINS OF A HUSTLA II
ASAD
YAYO V
Bred In The Game 2
S. Allen
THE STREETS WILL TALK II
By Yolanda Moore
SON OF A DOPE FIEND III
HEAVEN GOT A GHETTO III
SKI MASK MONEY III
By Renta
LOYALTY AIN'T PROMISED III
By Keith Williams
I'M NOTHING WITHOUT HIS LOVE II
SINS OF A THUG II
TO THE THUG I LOVED BEFORE II
IN A HUSTLER I TRUST II
By Monet Dragun

QUIET MONEY IV
EXTENDED CLIP III
THUG LIFE IV
By Trai'Quan
THE STREETS MADE ME IV
By Larry D. Wright
IF YOU CROSS ME ONCE III
ANGEL V
By Anthony Fields
THE STREETS WILL NEVER CLOSE IV
By K'ajji
HARD AND RUTHLESS III
KILLA KOUNTY IV
By Khufu
MONEY GAME III
By Smoove Dolla
JACK BOYS VS DOPE BOYS IV
A GANGSTA'S QUR'AN V
COKE GIRLZ II
COKE BOYS II
LIFE OF A SAVAGE V
CHI'RAQ GANGSTAS V
SOSA GANG III
BRONX SAVAGES II
BODYMORE KINGPINS II
By Romell Tukes
MURDA WAS THE CASE III
Elijah R. Freeman
AN UNFORESEEN LOVE IV

Cartel Money

BABY, I'M WINTERTIME COLD III
By Meesha

QUEEN OF THE ZOO III
By Black Migo
CONFESSIONS OF A JACKBOY III
By Nicholas Lock
KING KILLA II
By Vincent "Vitto" Holloway
BETRAYAL OF A THUG III
By Fre$h
THE MURDER QUEENS III
By Michael Gallon
THE BIRTH OF A GANGSTER III
By Delmont Player
TREAL LOVE II
By Le'Monica Jackson
FOR THE LOVE OF BLOOD III
By Jamel Mitchell
RAN OFF ON DA PLUG II
By Paper Boi Rari
HOOD CONSIGLIERE III
By Keese
PRETTY GIRLS DO NASTY THINGS II
By Nicole Goosby
PROTÉGÉ OF A LEGEND III
LOVE IN THE TRENCHES II
By Corey Robinson
IT'S JUST ME AND YOU II
By Ah'Million

Martell "T" Bolden

FOREVER GANGSTA III
By Adrian Dulan
GORILLAZ IN THE TRENCHES II
By SayNoMore
THE COCAINE PRINCESS VIII
By King Rio
CRIME BOSS II
Playa Ray
LOYALTY IS EVERYTHING III
Molotti
HERE TODAY GONE TOMORROW II
By Fly Rock
REAL G'S MOVE IN SILENCE II
By Von Diesel
GRIMEY WAYS IV
By Ray Vinci

Cartel Money

Available Now

RESTRAINING ORDER **I & II**
By CA$H & Coffee
LOVE KNOWS NO BOUNDARIES **I II & III**
By Coffee
RAISED AS A GOON I, II, III & IV
BRED BY THE SLUMS I, II, III
BLAST FOR ME I & II
ROTTEN TO THE CORE I II III
A BRONX TALE I, II, III
DUFFLE BAG CARTEL I II III IV V VI
HEARTLESS GOON I II III IV V
A SAVAGE DOPEBOY I II
DRUG LORDS I II III
CUTTHROAT MAFIA I II
KING OF THE TRENCHES
By Ghost
LAY IT DOWN **I & II**
LAST OF A DYING BREED I II
BLOOD STAINS OF A SHOTTA I & II III
By Jamaica
LOYAL TO THE GAME I II III
LIFE OF SIN I, II III
By TJ & Jelissa
BLOODY COMMAS I & II
SKI MASK CARTEL I II & III
KING OF NEW YORK I II,III IV V
RISE TO POWER I II III
COKE KINGS I II III IV V

Martell "T" Bolden
BORN HEARTLESS I II III IV
KING OF THE TRAP I II
By T.J. Edwards
IF LOVING HIM IS WRONG...I & II
LOVE ME EVEN WHEN IT HURTS I II III
By Jelissa
WHEN THE STREETS CLAP BACK I & II III
THE HEART OF A SAVAGE I II III IV
MONEY MAFIA I II
LOYAL TO THE SOIL I II III
By Jibril Williams
A DISTINGUISHED THUG STOLE MY
HEART I II & III
LOVE SHOULDN'T HURT I II III IV
RENEGADE BOYS I II III IV
PAID IN KARMA I II III
SAVAGE STORMS I II III
AN UNFORESEEN LOVE I II III
BABY, I'M WINTERTIME COLD I II
By Meesha
A GANGSTER'S CODE I &, II III
A GANGSTER'S SYN I II III
THE SAVAGE LIFE I II III
CHAINED TO THE STREETS I II III
BLOOD ON THE MONEY I II III
A GANGSTA'S PAIN I II III
By J-Blunt
PUSH IT TO THE LIMIT

Cartel Money

By Bre' Hayes

BLOOD OF A BOSS I, II, III, IV, V

SHADOWS OF THE GAME

TRAP BASTARD

By Askari

THE STREETS BLEED MURDER **I, II & III**

THE HEART OF A GANGSTA I II& III

By Jerry Jackson

CUM FOR ME I II III IV V VI VII VIII

An LDP Erotica Collaboration

BRIDE OF A HUSTLA **I II & II**

THE FETTI GIRLS **I, II& III**

CORRUPTED BY A GANGSTA I, II III, IV

BLINDED BY HIS LOVE

THE PRICE YOU PAY FOR LOVE I, II ,III

DOPE GIRL MAGIC I II III

By Destiny Skai

WHEN A GOOD GIRL GOES BAD

By Adrienne

THE COST OF LOYALTY I II III

By Kweli

A GANGSTER'S REVENGE **I II III & IV**

THE BOSS MAN'S DAUGHTERS I II III IV
V

A SAVAGE LOVE **I & II**

BAE BELONGS TO ME I II

A HUSTLER'S DECEIT I, II, III

WHAT BAD BITCHES DO I, II, III

SOUL OF A MONSTER I II III

KILL ZONE

Martell "T" Bolden
A DOPE BOY'S QUEEN I II III
TIL DEATH
By Aryanna
A KINGPIN'S AMBITON
A KINGPIN'S AMBITION **II**
I MURDER FOR THE DOUGH
By Ambitious
TRUE SAVAGE I II III IV V VI VII
DOPE BOY MAGIC I, II, III
MIDNIGHT CARTEL I II III
CITY OF KINGZ I II
NIGHTMARE ON SILENT AVE
THE PLUG OF LIL MEXICO II
CLASSIC CITY
By Chris Green
A DOPEBOY'S PRAYER
By Eddie "Wolf" Lee
THE KING CARTEL **I, II & III**
By Frank Gresham
THESE NIGGAS AIN'T LOYAL **I, II & III**
By Nikki Tee
GANGSTA SHYT **I II &III**
By CATO
THE ULTIMATE BETRAYAL
By Phoenix
Boss'n Up i , ii & IIi
By Royal Nicole
I LOVE YOU TO DEATH

Cartel Money
By Destiny J
I RIDE FOR MY HITTA
I STILL RIDE FOR MY HITTA
By Misty Holt
LOVE & CHASIN' PAPER
By Qay Crockett
TO DIE IN VAIN
SINS OF A HUSTLA
By ASAD
BROOKLYN HUSTLAZ
By Boogsy Morina
BROOKLYN ON LOCK I & II
By Sonovia
GANGSTA CITY
By Teddy Duke
A DRUG KING AND HIS DIAMOND I & II
III
A DOPEMAN'S RICHES
HER MAN, MINE'S TOO I, II
CASH MONEY HO'S
THE WIFEY I USED TO BE I II
PRETTY GIRLS DO NASTY THINGS
By Nicole Goosby
TRAPHOUSE KING **I II & III**
KINGPIN KILLAZ I II III
STREET KINGS I II
PAID IN BLOOD **I II**
CARTEL KILLAZ I II III
DOPE GODS I II
By Hood Rich

Martell "T" Bolden
LIPSTICK KILLAH **I, II, III**
CRIME OF PASSION I II & III
FRIEND OR FOE I II III
By Mimi
STEADY MOBBN' **I, II, III**
THE STREETS STAINED MY SOUL I II III
By Marcellus Allen
WHO SHOT YA **I, II, III**
SON OF A DOPE FIEND I II
HEAVEN GOT A GHETTO I II
SKI MASK MONEY I II
Renta
GORILLAZ IN THE BAY **I II III IV**
TEARS OF A GANGSTA I II
3X KRAZY I II
STRAIGHT BEAST MODE I II
DE'KARI
TRIGGADALE I II III
MURDAROBER WAS THE CASE I II
Elijah R. Freeman
GOD BLESS THE TRAPPERS I, II, III
THESE SCANDALOUS STREETS I, II, III
FEAR MY GANGSTA I, II, III IV, V
THESE STREETS DON'T LOVE NOBODY I,
II
BURY ME A G I, II, III, IV, V
A GANGSTA'S EMPIRE I, II, III, IV
THE DOPEMAN'S BODYGAURD I II
THE REALEST KILLAZ I II III

Martell "T" Bolden
LEVELS TO THIS SHYT I II
IT'S JUST ME AND YOU
By Ah'Million
KINGPIN DREAMS I II III
RAN OFF ON DA PLUG
By Paper Boi Rari
CONFESSIONS OF A GANGSTA I II III IV
CONFESSIONS OF A JACKBOY I II
By Nicholas Lock
I'M NOTHING WITHOUT HIS LOVE
SINS OF A THUG
TO THE THUG I LOVED BEFORE
A GANGSTA SAVED XMAS
IN A HUSTLER I TRUST
By Monet Dragun
CAUGHT UP IN THE LIFE I II III
THE STREETS NEVER LET GO I II III
By Robert Baptiste
NEW TO THE GAME I II III
MONEY, MURDER & MEMORIES I II III
By Malik D. Rice
LIFE OF A SAVAGE I II III IV
A GANGSTA'S QUR'AN I II III IV
MURDA SEASON I II III
GANGLAND CARTEL I II III
CHI'RAQ GANGSTAS I II III IV
KILLERS ON ELM STREET I II III
JACK BOYZ N DA BRONX I II III

Cartel Money

A DOPEBOY'S DREAM I II III

JACK BOYS VS DOPE BOYS I II III

COKE GIRLZ

COKE BOYS

SOSA GANG I II

BRONX SAVAGES

BODYMORE KINGPINS

By Romell Tukes

LOYALTY AIN'T PROMISED I II

By Keith Williams

QUIET MONEY I II III

THUG LIFE I II III

EXTENDED CLIP I II

A GANGSTA'S PARADISE

By Trai'Quan

THE STREETS MADE ME I II III

By Larry D. Wright

THE ULTIMATE SACRIFICE I, II, III, IV, V, VI

KHADIFI

IF YOU CROSS ME ONCE I II

ANGEL I II III IV

IN THE BLINK OF AN EYE

By Anthony Fields

THE LIFE OF A HOOD STAR

By Ca$h & Rashia Wilson

THE STREETS WILL NEVER CLOSE I II III

By K'ajji

CREAM I II III

THE STREETS WILL TALK

Cartel Money

By Khufu

MONEY GAME I II

By Smoove Dolla

A GANGSTA'S KARMA I II III

By FLAME

KING OF THE TRENCHES I II III

by GHOST & TRANAY ADAMS

QUEEN OF THE ZOO I II

By Black Migo

GRIMEY WAYS I II III

By Ray Vinci

XMAS WITH AN ATL SHOOTER

By Ca$h & Destiny Skai

KING KILLA

By Vincent "Vitto" Holloway

BETRAYAL OF A THUG I II

By Fre$h

THE MURDER QUEENS I II

By Michael Gallon

TREAL LOVE

By Le'Monica Jackson

FOR THE LOVE OF BLOOD I II

By Jamel Mitchell

HOOD CONSIGLIERE I II

By Keese

PROTÉGÉ OF A LEGEND I II

LOVE IN THE TRENCHES

By Corey Robinson

BORN IN THE GRAVE I II III

By Self Made Tay

Martell "T" Bolden
MOAN IN MY MOUTH
By XTASY
TORN BETWEEN A GANGSTER AND A
GENTLEMAN
By J-BLUNT & Miss Kim
LOYALTY IS EVERYTHING I II
Molotti
HERE TODAY GONE TOMORROW
By Fly Rock
PILLOW PRINCESS
By S. Hawkins

Cartel Money

BOOKS BY LDP'S CEO, CA$H

TRUST IN NO MAN
TRUST IN NO MAN 2
TRUST IN NO MAN 3
BONDED BY BLOOD
SHORTY GOT A THUG
THUGS CRY
THUGS CRY 2
THUGS CRY 3
TRUST NO BITCH
TRUST NO BITCH 2
TRUST NO BITCH 3
TIL MY CASKET DROPS
RESTRAINING ORDER
RESTRAINING ORDER 2
IN LOVE WITH A CONVICT
LIFE OF A HOOD STAR
XMAS WITH AN ATL SHOOTER

Printed in the USA
CPSIA information can be obtained
at www.ICGtesting.com
LVHW011541290124
770238LV00041B/909